McCOOL

McCOOL

Aidan Andrew Dun

GOLDMARK · UPPINGHAM · MMX

First published in 2010 by Goldmark, Uppingham, Rutland
Telephone 01572 821424
Goldmark publications may be viewed at
www.goldmarkbooks.com

ISBN 978-1-870507-67-7 (paperback)
ISBN 978-1-870507-68-4 (casebound)

Designed by Douglas Martin
Set in Joanna and Rosart
Printed and bound in Great Britain

For Kieran Francis Clarke

FRANK

A note on pronunciation

Tyg rhymes with 'intrigue'. This ancient name from the land of Hamlet has an extra 'e' in Danish, Tyge, and occasionally in English appears as 'Teague'.

1

News came on a grey morning. i
One of those defeated days
when spring is frigid, yawning
exhaustedly in a frozen haze;
unable to discover in mist
the many promises kissed
into the land with sunshine
only two weeks before, when fine
words were said by the Lord Sun
to his Lady, the green-eyed earth,
when Maytime first had her birth:
'I'll make you so warm, darling one,
I'll bring you golden summer joy.'
(What a brilliant solar playboy.)

At eight a Tornado GR4 ii
crossed the house so low to the ground
it troubled the exterior door,
made the coffee urn resound;
shook the glass breakfast table,
sent a shiver (it was unstable)
made of it a transparent drum:
see-through mirror-like tympanum.
Gala looked at her husband Parker
as the jet whined off across Rain Hill:
'He's down in the dirt.' There was a chill,
the day seemed immediately darker.
Then the red postvan roared straight
through the opened electronic gate.

The letter informed of deployment, iii
transference to the Lebanon.
The Queen's Deathshead regiment,
Royal Lancers, would be gone
in a fortnight, sudden clearance
due to new belligerence,
in view of theatre-escalation,
involvement of another nation.
Their commander, Col. Parker James,
would plan and mount black operations
with drone backup, combat-stations
skyside, smartfire, cosmic flames
at his beck and call. Gala waited.
Her man seemed truly checkmated.

She felt the first drop of rain, iv
knew his heart accelerated;
sensed his emotional pain,
understood he was elated.
They moved the table in together
out of unforeseeable weather,
two tall Caucasians in failed sunlight,
not saying much, the low-level flight
still covering them with abrasive
thunder, unearthly sound (as when
steel furnaces of hell slide open).
His 'Over soon' wasn't persuasive.
Inside, a tidal wave of tears
broke suddenly: Gala ran upstairs.

That night the sky seemed to lift; v
they loved frenziedly till dawn.
Song of the doves began to drift
through open windows; across the lawn
sunlight stretched warm fingers,
like a hand that sweetly lingers
on the hip of the tender earth,
horizon of warmth, giving birth
to new days. They loved again,
kissed slow lips, then slept till noon.
Not for years, since their honeymoon,
had these two drunk such champagne
from eachothers' mouths in passion.
(Parker'd strayed in a husband's fashion.)

Two weeks later in heavy rain vi
a Globemaster flew the regiment
out of Brize Norton, the huge jetplane
banking through grey firmament,
camouflaged ghost that slowly ceased
thundering away to the east.
Gala drove home in floods of tears;
the Isle of Purbeck heard her prayers.
Near the Great Rift Valley Parker
also prayed as Syrian missiles,
Scuds (of range three-fifty miles)
overflying the wartorn B'qaa
violated Lebanese airspace,
threatened his destination airbase.

In back-lanes of the peninsula, vii
Gala, in the big house that night
felt her grief bear down: insular
pain. Despairing, she took fright;
sat up late by the fireside
searching the Iliad, warbride.
'Fate: no one alive ever escaped
that; no hero or coward's reshaped
the destiny with which we're all born.'
Gala confided to her journal
what she'd not said to the Colonel:
'Already I'm the woman wartorn;
I pray you will not be hurt
yourself in the cruel desert.'

Fate masterminded an incident viii
which played out as the Lancers landed.
'This bit of Kleenex might just prevent
colds!' a squaddie joked, handed
facemask for the floodlit tarmac.
Still on alert (a semi-attack
'redstate' panic wasn't over yet,
high level biological threat)
the brand new outer tactical vest
with modular facepiece was dispensed
before deplaning, as the troop-fenced
Globemaster was EPD'd, progressed
through 'emergency personnel
descent' straight into a living hell.

The following day at sunrise ix
(as Parker trained in the warzone)
Gala on the coast walked under skies
burnished to a blue-gold bronze tone.
Sleepless, her slanting eyes, brown-green,
were huge mirrors in which could be seen
diametrically opposed rays,
colourings of different ways:
the bloodshot of remaining –
insomniac terrors of the night
alone – and an ultraviolet light,
Lulworth Cove's blue-gold retaining.
Morning spoke to Galatea.
Ocean whispered in her ear.

(She was half-Mediterranean, x
Italian blood on her mother's side.
The sea: Gala was semi-ocean,
her eyes seemed always open wide,
gazing at some expanse of water
down among fragrant, hotter
southern lands, turned to Provence,
Tuscany's coast of white lactescence;
where she would bathe slender hands,
her beautiful feet, go walking
in sandals, silver, not talking,
along the Tyrrhenian sands
beside Parker in the early days,
long ago, when love was ablaze.)

That afternoon she skyped Elaane; xi
they talked six hours, old friends.
'I don't expect a castle in Spain,
but frankly, sweetness, life depends
on getting out of this countryside.
Yesterday and I collide
constantly on this island,
not truly cut off, but sand-
circled, haunted with sadness.
I must rent this childless house,
creep back to London like a mouse
into a hole, otherwise: madness.'
(Gala was repeating word for word
good advice an hour earlier heard.)

'Gal, while Park's in the Lebanon, xii
don't stay isolated in Purbeck,
come back to town. With your man on
duty, back to work! Get a twin-deck
not far from the river, near me,
only thing you can do, honestly.
You'll weep your heart out in Lulworth Cove
where you and Parker made love,
so you said, in the olden days,
long ago in moonlight. Don't cry,
come to London; wipe your eyes dry:
you *can* walk out of this dark maze.'
Laane's gentle intonations soothed.
(Gala was, deep down, soon moved.)

'Your starchart's profoundly affected xiii
by the moon, in the manner
explained here in my *Collected*
Commentaries on the Arcana.'
(Laane interpreted cards, stars.)
'Your Venus, trine to his Mars,
offsets dangerous inclinations,
love of war. His red planet stations
itself retrograde. (I knew it.)
"Natives can be distant." You're ocean,
volatile, stormy with emotion,
moody and restless. I'll run through it
in London, lay out what's been said
on your lovely Indian bedspread.'

Telecom: a time-machine xiv
taken for granted. (Like too many
miracles.) Do thoughts travel between
Swanage, Pimlico, without any
telecommunication link,
automatically? Think,
two hours by train. Impossible!
No trembling of an ossicle
inside the tympanic cavity
without that telephonic
'*Ring, ring*' (which is transchronic,
bending time with relativity).
Gala could not have travelled
that day, she was so unravelled.

Laane saw the tears, heard the tone, xv
immediately sympathized. (A heart
tortured, troubled, lost and alone,
tested at midnight.) With starchart
flew silver Macbook Pro to Purbeck:
down the leylines with her tarot-deck.
Galatea came to her senses.
Destiny: don't fight it! Defences
went down; readings from the cards
(Spread of Memphis) preceded Homer:
song of a warlord beachcomber
dreaming his return home, regards
ever-sweeping the 'wine-dark sea',
turning from the land's 'solidity'.

One month later Dorset disappeared. xvi
The weight of the house was lifted,
as if a secret force, some weird
supernatural wind had drifted
through the world, floated it away.
Gala's slim shoulders again lay
down. Comforted, she quit crying,
M-skyped Parker often, ceased lying
to her husband, saying she was fine;
lost her cool, cursed the desert-war;
screamed: '*Screw* the idiot auditor!'
(The censor on the military line.)
He was crushed to realize her pain;
natural heroics were inane.

'Babe, of course you're thrilled to be back *xvii*
at trendy Aesthetican, glad to
launch an editorial attack.
(Aunt Wendy said you were mad to
move to London suddenly,
daft bitch.) If it were humanly
possible I would be with you.'
(Hiatus.) 'Parker, is it true?'
'You mean about biological;
you know I can't talk about that.
The B'qaa is sealed, a stray cat
couldn't jump, it's technological.'
His tanned face blurred; digital whine
hit the connection. 'Darling mine,'

'Take care.' Gala went off to work, *xviii*
a lump in her throat. (Gameplan:
to immerse herself in berserk
activity, career woman
insanity, mind-numbing grind,
anything to leave the war behind.)
For Parker it wasn't so easy;
several of his guys were queasy.
One young private's midnight screams
confirmed aversion syndrome:
the cooler-heater vest, cuddlesome
trilaminate friend. His bad dreams
were low-mooding the other men.
Col. James was there for them, as when

He led nineteen-year-old soldiers xix
across nocturnal desert terrain,
through hostile southwestern Syria's
high risk country, in freezing mountain
conditions. His primary goal?
To give each combatant *self-control*.
(Clearly a man follows orders,
penetrating foreign borders,
clad in computerized armour,
hi-tech science-fiction knight
still carrying the good fight
through the dry sand to Dumayr.)
Col. James expected something more;
he placed self-reliance to the fore.

The private's helpless nightmare? xx
He was trapped under a noon sun
with vest-malfunctioning-software,
cooked like a frankfurter in a bun.
The torso-hugging tubes mistreated
him; far from cooling, superheated.
He couldn't look at the damned jacket
without breaking out in a cold sweat.
'Fried egg', 'deep freeze', he called it.
(There had been some negative trials,
rumours flew round after denials;
designers had twice recalled it.)
Parker took the sick man to Beirut;
spent a night sucking forbidden fruit.

Old infidelities of war: xxi
a saddened, disillusioned world winks.
'It's me, the whore, they're fighting for',
sings Helen, 'I'm as the world thinks.'
Her Grecian beauty on the towers,
goddess of moonlight and sunflowers,
self-hating as Gala, truly cursed
when she called herself the worst
slut because her wandering eye,
warm (with greenish-brown backlit)
on some good-looking man alit,
focussed on some incidental guy.
Parker felt himself lowered, cheapened.
The private seemed to cool down. Deepened.

A hot night in a Beirut cathouse xxii
appeared to kill the bugaboo;
overheating desert rat and 'spouse'
did the flophouse bedroom boogaloo,
that oldest dance of ill-repute:
Enkidu and the prostitute,
the wildman and his knowing 'wife'.
Parker's doubts about the strife,
the justness of the war, reflected
(as he romanced *his* young harlot,
cute, nubile soft-porn starlet)
the sense of a dirty act infected.
Gala hunted with her gaze so pure,
green eyes full of innocent allure.

2

i

June in the vast metropolis.
The city like a sinking ship
dives in flame through an abyss
of houses, towers; seems to slip
down an incline of despair,
through a filthy atmosphere
of getting as opposed to giving.
(Can these be said to be the living,
who drag themselves through the streets,
briefcases and laptops supercharged
with that worldview which has enlarged
the vested interest of elites?)
Look, isn't that the great Titanic
submerged beneath the North Atlantic?

ii

London Town of the oligarchs:
it's so elegant by the river;
and if you live close to great parks,
such pleasure. It's a life-giver
to be anywhere near greenery,
otherworldly scenery,
waterbirds that glide across your cares,
suave, white, unruffled millionaires.
(Swans, among aquatic avians,
seem the yachts of the feathered races.)
Equity traders don't change places
with dangerous Rastafarians
whose meditations in the night
cool down a neighbourhood gunfight.

Their verdant city is far away iii
from these barrens of the town,
dustbowls of inner decay,
zones of ultramodern meltdown.
Fogs of marijuana hang here,
toxic fumes in octane air.
As gangs loot, as the war drags on,
summer rasps the name: 'Lebanon.'
Here the red mist is intense,
it's WWIII on television,
squad cars, icecream vans, in collision
(all sorts of other disagreements),
police sirens, *Teddy Bears' Picnic*,
blowing through a wilderness of brick.

Distorted chimes announce now iv
(Francis Bacon canvas in 3D)
the cross-section of a frozen cow
in a block of ice (riddle-me-ree)
pulled through the street to the sound of bells.
(From which of forty-eight-thousand hells
does this hallucination arise?)
Pale children of the highrise
tenement towerblocks congregate,
worship at this mobile shrine:
cult of the unholy bovine.
Let us hope they are too late
to suck cold udders of communion
at the icecream van of reunion.

A drunken male rages from the blocks. v
A woman's bark is terminated
with a body-blow which shocks
dirty windows, desecrated
by filthy swear words flying.
Reluctantly light is trying
to enter a darkened room;
our infrared night-vision zoom
camera scans the shabby flat:
the crackpipe on the plastic dresser,
the pornomags of the aggressor:
realm of the proletariat.
A victim's screams are hidden by chimes
grinding from the street a hundred times.

It is each day and every hour vi
she taunts again her idle man;
her 'unemployable' turns sour
in the heat. A half-broken fan
turns round with a death rattle,
goes on, like her sarcastic prattle,
blowing hot air about in hell:
'So why don't you sign up, Del,
too hard for the armed forces?
Jonjo's in the Royal Deathshead,
my kid brother, nineteen, 'nuff said.'
Such conversations and discourses
fill the sky with poison haze.
There's nothing else to talk of these days.

An unspecified presence vii
hovers in the town's atmosphere,
as if some psychic recrudescence
haunted, just behind the heavy air,
an angry tribal father-of-all
demanding blood, on the wall
his scarlet writing; in the sky
his 'Soldier's Autobiography'
(script of vapours) dimming light:
contrails of the troop transporters
(with embedded war reporters)
eclipsing the sun with lies. Tonight
they'll be recruiting in the cheap bars:
'We're gonna fly that flag to Mars.'

'Come, someone I want you to meet, viii
not a million miles from here.
Of course you can travel in the heat
(not to the Red Planet, so near).
Let's go, I'll introduce you to Tyg,
he's in his studio, not a league
from where we find ourselves this morning.
You're wary, you've had a warning
about the "diseased opacity"
of my friend?' 'Well, Aesthetican
first named him "Armageddon man"
because of his mordacity,
the way his works reflect on death,
visions more bloody than Macbeth.'

(Thunder, lightning!) Well I introduced ix
Gala to the painter Tyg McCool.
Even then he was traduced,
called an anti-glamorizing fool
because of *Battlefield in Helmand,*
Hero Carcase. Yet in demand,
since that lie which shows us truth –
art – might be offensive and uncouth,
but without it glossy magazines,
mock-intellectual publications,
would have no real implications,
could only be for boudoir queens.
There was a dark halo around Tyg.
(Fame's limelight and foggy intrigue.)

I took Gala and her friend Elaane x
over to De Beauvoir Town,
out to the Tower in Aquitaine,
ultramodern canalside godown
where the painter had his top deck:
his 'floor of light' above the wreck,
the cataclysm of Hackney.
A heated afternoon turned rainy,
a lift exhaled the smoke of weed;
mist from the sluggish waterway
brought to the balcony a bouquet:
urban perfume of summer indeed.
With Laane I stood and sniffed the air.
Tyg had a chat with Galatea.

For some time she had been set xi
on interviewing the war artist.
(Her glossy was casting a dragnet
through the art world; smartest
people took an interest in McCool.)
His canvases showed the cruel
grinding visage of unglorified
desert warfare, where on every side
sand seemed ready to drink blood,
the body fluid of all mankind,
to suck down in the landmined
wastes, absorb a red flashflood.
Crimson Dunes was such a piece;
another was just titled: *Decease*.

The shock of a McCool was almost xii
always sanguinary, critics said.
In *Hero Carcase* you saw raw, roast
carrion, sundried and widespread,
swollen black balloons of flesh,
erupting from Hieronymus Bosch-
like treatments of decomposition.
(The painter had his own permission
to probe the death of a brave man,
who cared from what side: a fist's a fist.
Tyg posed as photojournalist
up along the border with Iran
near Halabjah, got his takes
east of the Sulaymaniyah lakes.)

Who knows what was talked about? xiii
When Laane and I did breeze in
McCool and Galatea without
seeming tense or ill at ease in
eachother's company were silent,
facing that insanely violent
masterpiece *Battlefield in Helmand*
with its slain prone in the red sand.
Reclined on Kunodi lounge
the living sprawled opposite the dead,
silent also on their deathbed.
One split-second Laane had to range
widely in her mind for words to float
into the void. (Where was the right note?)

Her judgment, always astute, xiv
detected an elusive balance
in the air, as McCool rolled a zoot,
an existential double dance.
'You first showed this at White Cube, right?'
'Yeah that was a calamitous night.
Predictably I ran my big mouth,
everyone there, north and south,
the Dia, the Metropolitan,
the Guggenheim. Suddenly
two military types corner me,
point to *Helmand*, say: "For God's sake, man,
did you do that?" And there, amid
crowds I shout: "NO, I DIDN'T. *YOU* DID!"'

I hadn't seen Gala laugh for years *xv*
(I knew her before she married).
Both girls were reduced to tears,
yet Galatea's laughter carried
a bitter tone behind her delight.
We drifted down to a winebar quite
nearby, along the Ball's Pond Road.
Conversation pleasantly flowed
till Laane – probably on second drink –
rang bells with one of her answers,
mentioned the Queen's Royal Lancers.
It was out before an eye could blink:
'This war without end, can it be won?
Gala's husband's in the Lebanon.'

'Her Majesty's Royal Deathshead? *xvi*
Specialists in black operations;
that military thoroughbred
for doomsday situations?
I'd like to meet him.' I studied Tyg
(with a reputation for blitzkrieg
lightning strikes himself) watching Gala,
unreadable as the Cabbala,
aquiline silhouette, mobile jaw,
stubbled, working. More intent,
closer toward her he leant
as if he had not seen her before,
adrift in her eyes' greenish hue,
many lightyears from an interview.

Rain swept the Angel Islington xvii
as we put the girls in a black cab.
According to her ringtone
McCool had been able to grab
Gala's number in the downpour.
(Her mobile rang as he slammed the door.)
He texted her as we had a drink
in our hangout 'The Big Pink':
'Galatea. Love 2 link nxt week!'
Then, distant, preoccupied, pensive,
he seemed almost apprehensive;
in his expression an oblique
disengagement. I left him alone
(fiddling about with his phone).

Nightwalking the canal eastward xviii
after midnight, the cloudburst
raised the water level. Onward
we lurched via sometimes submersed
concrete shorelines where reflection
merged the cityscape, on inspection
blended water-sky with tower-lights.
McCool delivered soundbytes.
He'd just returned from Baghdad,
city of walls, street against street,
the Tigris full of floating man-meat.
He'd seen brutalities, Stalingrad,
darkness into darkness crash;
corpses in a stinking mishmash,

Strange shoals of infernal fishmen *xix*
bloating in the shadowy river,
arm in arm swimming away. (Often
I've remembered McCool's endeavour
that night, with language, to recapture
all his dark, hellish, rapture:
his visions of Sumeria.)
He was suddenly wearier,
sadder in life than ever before.
(We pushed against driving rain;
there was only never-ending pain.)
'In Iran an orphan girl named "whore"
hung from a crane in the night sky:
a thousand cursed her with one cry.'

'Genocide by indoctrination, *xx*
here military, there religious.
Propaganda, hallucination,
make all of us (outrageous!)
seem inherently violent,
naturally belligerent.
It's a collective death kiss.'
'*Be* the change you wish to see in this
world.' (I quoted Gandhi's pearled
wisdom in the rain.) 'Come to birth
civilizations of heaven on earth.'
(Words through mystic cloudburst swirled,
in the painter another poet
beneath the surface, just below it.)

Under a span in De Beauvoir xxi
we held up for the duration.
In the deluge a lightning scar
ripped the night of transfiguration;
disappeared the Queensbridge Road.
As water on water overflowed,
tactile and substantive vanished:
solid land was hidden, banished.
A thundercloud sent out a fork
which stabbed the city in its side
eastward, in its skyscrapered pride.
That put an end to all our talk!
As the storm continued its harangue,
amid the thunder Tyg's phone rang.

He read a text from Galatea: xxii
'No interview, sorry, truly.'
Elegant McCool (chessplayer,
womanizer) never unduly
concerned with individual pieces,
more keen on overall increases,
leaps of power, the abstract game
(a dime a dozen women came)
would normally have raised a palm,
shrugged shoulders, dropped a blue joke,
directed inward some minor poke,
made light. Instead he showed alarm.
Queens and pawns, it seemed he'd understood,
are different, though made of one wood.

3 Whispering low a Myrmidon i
drone supercopter disappeared
over the dark Anti-Lebanon.
At midnight, a second machine reared
from the moonless night of Riyaq,
unpiloted too, also pitch black,
on board a Deathshead kidnap team.
Leaning out into the airstream
Col. James watched airbase shrink,
calm, breathing away nervousness
(cool pro of clandestine services),
one eye to the drone's screenlink.
Though they'd had less than a month to train
his men were *on* for Al Qaryatayn.

Clad in sombre dragonskin, ii
armed with rarefaction wavegun,
wearing trilaminate vests within
outer scale armour (no fun
if the software failed and roasted you)
these, hand-picked, were Parker's boasted few.
Seven ghost-troopers: his strongarm squad.
Heads hidden in the 'helmet of God'
advanced combat Headgear Four Thousand
they seemed humanoid scorpions,
not men; futuristic champions
loyal to some Lord of Belowland;
resembled soldier-insects, vast bean-
pod skulls nodding before their Queen.

Mission: to grab three 'superglow' iii
nuclear men from Al Qaryatayn
fifty miles over the Eastern Plateau.
Intention: to ascertain
the hotstrike power of Syria.
(Recently, Western hysteria
with the advent of Damascus
as terror's battering ram, focus
for 'fear of a dirty bomb
in the arsenal of a rogue state'.
Some had felt it wasn't too late
to confront 'extremist Islam'
in its new capital. Madman John
McCain invaded Lebanon.)

'Cain's returned to Heliopolis,' iv
they said in the cafes of Beirut.
(Referring to the metropolis
buried deep by ancient repute
under the Platform of Baalbek,
City of the Sun: hidden deck
of megalithic twelve-hundred-ton
blocks laid down by Adam's son
before the Flood. Superstitions
concerning stonework so immense
blended speculation, commonsense,
the Titan myth of folk traditions,
science-fiction.) Some said of McCain:
'He's back to murder us *again*.'

Parker tasted metal in his mouth, v
sniffed octane of rotorblades, sickly.
The B'qaa valley, running north-south
through Baalbek, dropped away quickly.
Pixels flashed. The drone relayed
signal via skystation, stayed
motionless, in locked position,
for full target-acquisition
over sleeping Al Qaryatayn.
A fighter ace, ex-Vietnam,
piloting the UAV (Grand Slam
missiles, four Smartfires to rain)
sucked on coke in a US fort
undersand, in zone of support.

Parker's stealth on autopilot vi
crossed the M1 Damascus highway
in whispermode, radar-silent, not
more than a shadow in the skyway,
blowing northeast on an eerie breath:
lethal seed full of black death.
(The nonpiloted robochopper
was still a conversation-stopper
in military circles. Special
ops, which retrospectively
'never happened', protectively
considered total silence crucial.
Loose-lipped stickjockeys were bad news.
Nonexistent pilots wore no shoes.)

Visual contact with Al Qaryatayn *vii*
(grid of lights on the desert floor,
faint matrix in a dark terrain)
put the team on maximum 'go for'.
The drone could 'see' the installation:
the reactor in preparation,
sinister plutonium-house
camouflaged in cat and mouse
atmospheres of subterfuge.
(Was enrichment – yellowcake – complete?
The Royal Deathshead would not retreat
without the brains of the centrifuge.)
High-res images onscreen
revealed to Col. James the unseen.

Programmed touchdown near an olive grove *viii*
west of the site was smooth going.
Parker transmitted 'code mauve'
to the drone in the clouds, showing
'standby' to launch the first strike.
He and his men made a short hike
via sparse cover on stony ground;
at outer fence had a shake-round.
Col. James then signalled 'code green'.
A filling station (edge-of-town)
went up in flames. Skyfire came down.
The night exploded with tangerine
tongues of petroleum combustion:
Phase One, Operation Compulsion.

Personnel from the complex *ix*
raced to the blaze, sirens howling.
Digitally jamming the fence-checks
Parker and black squad went prowling
into the dormitory zone
(leaving the reactor alone)
entered a ventilation duct,
vast pipe which silently sucked
night air, cool, into the system.
Belly-crawling in cold drafts,
labyrinthine aluminium shafts
proved claustrophobic for them.
Fears in the men were triggered.
Col. James had the maze figured.

They broke out on the second floor, *x*
eight black bugs emerging from the wall;
found themselves in a long corridor
leading westward to the dining-hall.
(The other way, round to the right,
sleeping quarters were up one flight.)
Splitting to four pairs, moving fast,
Roddy and Jonjo, first and last,
stood sentry at the double exit
as six black shapes crashed three doors down.
A man of science in dressing-gown
collapsed, threatened to vomit,
defecated in his pyjamas.
There were other little dramas.

Jonjo, stationed at 'point minaret', *xi*
visor down, wavegun on 'ready',
communicating through headset,
warned of unexpected steady
callsigns of the Republican Guard
streaming in his listenhard.
If not in the facility now
they were nearby; to disallow
access to the main stairwells
they'd have to move inside a minute:
jump to the next phase fast to win it.
Abductees and infidels
(two of the former scummed in sick)
made it to the stairhead doublequick.

Controlling heartbeat, Parker *xii*
gave the order to descend.
Halfway down a risktaker
ran in and met a sudden end,
filled the entrance with haunting cry
(takedown one) the first to die.
Ben Flynn's wavegun only coughed,
the sound it made was so soft.
Superbullets split the cranium,
the wavegun hissing out its shots,
the man's brains making giant blots
red on the white wall. 'Titanium,'
murmured Flynn through his headset.
(He meant the barrel of his black pet.)

In the lobby on the ground floor xiii
(abducted whitecoats groaning)
they were raked through the glass door,
shattered. There was no postponing
phase two, Operation Compulsion:
climactic hyperconvulsion!
(Not to be avoided, it seemed,
this part of the nightraid was schemed
only if the going was tough,
a drastic get-out strategy
for a serious catastrophe.)
Colonel James deemed it bad enough;
from his laptop actioned 'code red'.
The drone fighter ace, on centrespread,

Folded Playboy, clicked on 'fire': xiv
a Grand Slam fell out of the sky.
Night became a funeral pyre.
'With the glance of a laser eye
an electric bolt of Zeus
flew down to suddenly reduce
earth to incinerated ashes ...'
(The land remembers other clashes:
the Hundred-hander of the Titans
leading the wars of the elder gods
when the whole cosmos was at odds.
And now the cedar forest frightens
Enkidu as Gilgamesh faces
the watchman of the mountain places.)

A thud as if the dead moon *xv*
had fallen onto the living earth;
a flash as if the sun's balloon
of hydrogen had given birth
to a universal fireball:
the reactor's waisted eight-floor-tall
cooling tower exploded.
(A laser guided Slam unloaded
ruination onto the structure.)
Dark turned sea of luminous red:
radioactive smoke widespread.
Against the detonation's rupture
Parker ordered: 'Circle formation.'
Then, out of the conflagration,

From the doorway's frame of shards, *xvi*
through the compound's anarchy,
crossfire from Republican Guards
(in a scene from Titanomachy)
shielding the half-dead scientists,
ashen prisoners in their midst,
Deathshead squad in dragonskin
exited as one man. Till Ben Flynn
took a deep hit in the right thigh,
collected at perimeter fence
some rocket-propelled ordnance
(bringing down the black-clad samurai).
Two Lancers pulled him through barbed wire,
dragged him on their shoulders under fire.

With lightning-struck reactor xvii
in the background – Babel tower
burning – with speed as main factor,
they raced with superman willpower
through the deepening firestorm.
Hot blazing air seemed to deform
everything; their way was difficult
to make out through smoky tumult:
trees spontaneously igniting,
the atmosphere, an ocean of flame.
Jonjo, half in a video game,
half in the grim world of real fighting,
fully maxed-out now his cooler vest,
appreciated, yeah, it was best.

Bullets bounced off dragonskin, xviii
(the outer hide of Baphomet).
A groove was going on within,
a soundtrack in his ultra-helmet:
'When we ride on our enemies.'
(Or something from The Fugees.)
Pushy beats made him supreme:
he was back in his bedroom dream
playstationing through adolescence;
only lacking a green zoot
to make him hotter in pursuit,
he was virtual belligerence
clad in scale armour, reptilian,
childlike, the true post-civilian.

Satnav on helmet-visor *xix*
guided Parker west with his team.
(He stopped to jab a tranquillizer
into Flynn, semiconscious, extreme
pain from shattered thigh taking
over the man's mind, making
him a helpless liability.)
Out of the zone of hostility
shepherding his military flock
(explosions in the night behind
making the dry earth seem to grind)
from nowhere an electric shock
passed through his body, and a blow
laid him on the ground head-to-toe.

Galatea spoke as he hit dust. *xx*
'World War Three' (she seemed to be saying
through sounds of battlezone bloodlust,
military machines manslaying)
'is madness … normalized … forever.'
Dream-faint she struggled to deliver
(pronouncing slowly) the words again;
as a white heat and a black rain
engulfed his scapula: agony.
(Parker only regained proper
consciousness in the robochopper
under anodyne monotony.)
A fluke bullet had flown between
silicon scales of his bodyscreen.

From the sting he'd lost much blood. *xxi*
A sniper on the ridge had caught him
in nightsights as he'd led black squad
down to the olive grove by dim
light of dawn: his left shoulder
lay torn open. Life-leaseholder
still (with the contract of clay)
he thought of someone far away.
Col. 'PJ' torturously smiled.
The dragon was not omnipotent.
A bulletproof skin was efficient
but fatality was domiciled
yet within the human animal.
Parker felt a cold steel decimal

Point inside him where the bullet stayed. *xxii*
Death had tried to cut him down to size,
slash his life to a fraction, grade
him back to a percentage, revise
the standing of an 'immortal',
drag him through a dark portal
into the enigma of the grave.
He gazed at Flynn guiltily (brave
man of war) clear amputation-case.
Then, slipping from consciousness, saw
Gala outstretched on a wooden floor.
One tear tracked the colonel's dusty face.
As the sun rose on sleeping Riyaq
a subjective universe went black.

4

The night of the ghost operation, i
as Parker crossed Syrian airspace,
in dense London precipitation
Gala and Elaane gave chase
to a taxicab on Upper Street.
Tyg and companion also beat
the rainy pavement in pursuit
(more of the girls than the driver's route).
As the heavy door was slammed
(the storm put in its external place,
the bad weather told to hide its face)
Gala's mobile rang with that damned
'*Air on a G String*' which sounded
more parody, music dumbfounded.

She cut the flimsy ringtone short ii
(as Father Bach turned in his grave)
under stroboscopic streetlights brought
her thumb to bear on 'T' (save)
and so on. The monosyllabic
name entered, a million electric
wonders of the night flashed out.
Gala gazed in wet glass without
conscious orientation thinking.
The city had tears in its eyes.
With Parker, under other skies,
she was near danger, a sinking
feeling in her secret heart of hearts.
Elaane sensed it through her mystic arts.

'Were you aware that "the London Bach", iii
Johann's youngest, most talented son
lies buried in what's become a park,
a magic island in Kings Cross? One
early morning let's go there.' Gala –
feeling like the frightened impala
when lion, cheetah and hyena
hunt her at night in the savannah –
turned and glanced across at Laane.
(Her friend was making smalltalk
to save the dove from the fast hawk.)
'I knew that Rimbaud and Verlaine
lived there. And I've heard other things
about the place called Cross of Kings'

'From poets.' Yet she was discomposed. iv
And now she asked her pal to explain:
'Elaane. Why – O why? – was it disclosed
about Parker, sweet featherbrain?
Now any interview will be just…
Who needs their private life discussed?
If we talk art, share views of war
from vantages more abstract, more
philosophical, what's *my* distress?'
Laane turned a flippin' somersault:
'Gal, you're being difficult.
Yeah okay, my stupid fault I guess;
but look on the upside, you've met Tyg:
now your writing can go major league.'

‘Run with the wolf.’ Gala sat still, v
gazed through tears at her wedding-ring,
began to feel dizzy, slightly ill.
Cheesy strains, ‘*Air on a G String*’,
filled the cab, made them giggle;
there seemed no reason now to niggle.
‘Galatea. Love 2 link nxt week!’
(Crimson tints rose to someone’s cheek.)
Wheels hissed where the road’s camber
curved down to the flooded gutters
filled with raindrop’s endless splutters.
Traffic lights turned from red to amber.
‘Sweetness, sorry, come back to mine,
have a chat, drink a glass of wine?’

An apartment near the river. vi
Electric green and low yellow
sidelighting. A tuft of vetiver,
nearby a tall dusty cello
standing among long grasses.
(It would not seem that taut passes,
bowings of tension had relayed
harmonies of some old serenade
from this abandoned instrument
recently, forgotten and dust-clad.)
A wall-length photograph: Trinidad.
Brilliant coastline, blue firmament,
beautiful; but the panorama
from river-wall: Rousseau’s *Snakecharmer*.

‘Read me some Homer.’ And Gala, sad, vii
randomly opened her translation,
read from her beloved Iliad:
‘No mortal man of procreation
ever had such armour on his back.
Look at this! See the flashback
reflection’s brighter than the sun.
Ransack earth, this can’t be outdone.
Look what the cosmic gods have made.
I tell you, I’m going to battle,
and on my chest I’ll buckle
bronze plates of superhuman aid,
now, as my friend’s body rots away,
as flies ride his wounds, today.’

She murmured two words, slid to the ground; viii
her forehead travelled bare wood.
(Two names of similar sound.)
Hot bitter tears of her wifehood
splashed onto the poetry book
(lost in the rug) as meaning took
hold. Her wineglass went sideways;
nosebridge, *wet*, was crushed; in a daze
she felt cold floorboards hurting her:
Laane’s arms supporting, strengthened.
On Chesterfield she slowly lengthened,
whispered of what was haunting her:
‘Parker changed deeply in Kosovo
when Pat was killed, then came the affair.’

She faltered, just comprehensible; ix
slurred and muddled what she said.
'God, so distant and invisible,
tonight he could be – Parker – dead.'
Laane, always the philosopher,
listened in silence (bless her).
'Patrick's loss seemed to fester in Park;
he never really came back from the dark
winter when his friend was killed.
(Terrible deaths become obsessions.)
He still has post-traumatic visions,
flashbacks to that tragic minefield
near Pec. Parker's memory's a hell
full of what Homer has to tell.'

'Gala, sweetness, all can change. x
(Remember the Renaissance
took the Hundred Years' War to arrange,
or *rearrange*, recircumstance.)
PJ needs help, that's for sure.
He's stuck in a revolving door:
don't worry, we'll get him right.'
(Laane's face is set alight;
a believer in the Golden Age,
does she know what it takes to get there?
She understands what joy is met there:
Elaane is a scholar and a sage.)
'Fear gets trapped in the amygdala,
Gal. There's a battlefield modeller

Stateside: exposure therapy. *xi*
Emotional photographs retouched
at the source of pain. Parks could walk free
out of that future-machine. Detached,
cold, he's spiritually damaged.
Loss of his friend has ravaged
him, left him frightened to come close
since, as he'd naturally suppose,
you're next in life's crazy roulette.'
(Laane had a telling way with words;
sometimes she counselled lovebirds.)
'Think how lonely it must get
walking the streets with such injuries,
through apocalyptic auguries.'

About midnight they crept to bed. *xii*
'Thanks for staying over, my love.'
Laane kissed her friend: 'Goodnight, airhead.'
Thunder wobbled through the sky above,
Gala fiddled with her mobile,
then, after an elapse, a good while,
sent a message, slightly woolly.
'No interview, sorry, truly.'
Instantly regretted the cool
negative, superdistant tone,
wished she could reclaim, backloan,
empty words again, felt a fool.
(But there's no way to amend
once you've pressed the button marked 'send'.)

She lay awake in the rainstorm xiii
examining a strange day backward;
small hours seemed to transform
everything on the chequerboard.
(Serotonin clarity
revealed superreality.)
She felt her heart's inclination,
conceded her admiration
her liking for Tyg McCool,
most turned-on (and best-dressed) man
in counterculture: strangely blessed man.
Time to reinvent her golden rule,
come face to face with the truth of war?
His visions ran you through the core.

Left you silent; could lay bare xiv
(these dark, horrific onslaughts)
say what the world could not declare,
cry out its forbidden thoughts.
Surely everything transacted
on the present still impacted.
She 'stepped off the kerb', woke with bump,
drifted again, took another jump
into a dream of waterways.
Slant rain drove on the skylight's pane,
distant sirens caterwauled. Elaane
turned and mumbled: 'Someone who betrays ...'
(If only it had been kept secret
about Parker, not said yet.)

Raindrops accelerated and went *xv*
skating on wet glass, winged away
on wild night-flights, emissaries sent
gliding across the dark as spray.
Flurries and pearling of the rain
(washing-clear of the day's stain)
soothed Gala: she came to the border
controlled by that black marauder
who invades waking existence,
taking hostages, putting them under
in sleep's hidden world of wonder,
robbing them of commonsense.
She surrendered; and was airlifted.
Into dreamland Gala drifted.

London slumbers: a million streets *xvi*
like empty stages floodlit
wait silently beneath concrete
tiers and balconies. (Some pit
lets out a blood-curdling roar.)
An old actor at a stage door
whispers to a rundown tart:
he's missed his entrance, blown his part.
Now this sad pair, arm in arm,
dissolve into city shadows
drinking to their failed tomorrows.
(Stridor of a burglar alarm
suggests an ironic wedding bell.)
Through night rain tottering, farewell.

Pan to rebel criminal xvii
hooded in sorrowful depression,
haunting dim corners, subliminal
fear of the urban in possession,
in control of somatic language,
crack-fiend of the town's bondage,
hyped and nervy demon – tense –
one more victim of the immense
facelessness of modern living.
(Citizen control television
ogles with cold inquisition,
metallic eyelids unforgiving,
narrows now to focus upon
that obscure con, this diamond don.)

Deep in some labyrinthine club xviii
financiers and their gold-digging
platinum-blonde females rub
shoulders with champagne-swigging
minor English aristocracy.
(Cocaine, in ascendancy,
disappears up haute monde noses:
high life's unregulated doses.)
The talk is dreary and mundane:
someone's prenuptial agreement
comes under the most vehement
public scrutiny; loss and gain
hold the key to such exclusive rooms.
(Let us leave these monsters to their glooms.)

Over the sparkling metropolis *xix*
eastward are bohemian sectors.
(Does the Corona Borealis,
brilliant with starry stellar scriptures,
shine any brighter than these buildings,
these giant electric-green hill-things
scintillating in the atmosphere?)
The city is crowned just over here:
nocturnal heap of decked jewels,
spangled towers, electric splendour.
Beyond, a poet, pale and slender,
somewhere plunges through mind-pools,
big rivers of imagination,
bent to his poem, his creation.

The nightwind is the tread of his muse *xx*
on the tops of the houses passing.
A soft way she has with no shoes
carrying his light, never pausing,
restless angel transporting
beauty though rain's distorting.
Waterdroplets make the strapping,
the laces of her slipping-slapping
sandals, as she comes dancing
with the rainfall's ever-whirling
pitter-patter beads swirling
through gutters: mind-entrancing!
(Rhythms of the storm at night
up in the rooftops out of sight.)

Barefoot moonrays danced above xxi
Gala as, for once, she slept deeply.
(Unimaginable way of love,
why do you lead so steeply
always onwards and upwards?
Lovers are such lazy laggards.)
Smiling, still shedding tears, dawn,
transparent and half-naked morn,
walked in ricochets and reflections.
A wet night began to give way
before first brazen horns of day.
A symphony, its closing sections
plaintive, slow, its movement grand,
played out in the night's last stand.

At breakfast on the balcony: xxii
'I'm booking for Sardinia;
this summer is passing so bleakly.
I'll stay with John and Eugenia,
no editorials, weeks swimming.
I must escape this city, swarming
with warmongers and politicians
under painful weather conditions,
get far away.' 'Babe, you're right,
go melt into some white coastline,
find the continuous sunshine,
maybe look for your inner light.'
Gala eyed her mystic friend Elaane;
from her phone lastminuted her plane.

5 Twenty-four hours later, midday, i
dressing for Gatwick, Macbook rang.
A deep voice said in a cordial way:
'General Julian Lang
calling Mrs Galatea James.'
One split-second she saw black flames;
yet from the tone knew Parker living.
(With subduement of misgiving
she heard the soft-spoken general
point by point break his bad news.
Her request he hastened to refuse.
Most regrettably, a personal
visit to the Lebanese warzone:
something she would have to postpone.)

She sat, a queen inside her castle ii
besieged, suitcases surrounding,
cried her moats full (existential
terror at her portcullis pounding).
Where she'd fallen two nights before
on the wooden length of the floor
she fell again; her flight soon taking
off in Sussex, she collapsed shaking,
alone with fear. (Last minute gates
closed, aircraft rose into the sun,
free of cloud.) She remained as one
crushed underneath mental states
comparable to death, so quiet,
catatonic (like poor Juliet).

She phoned the military hospital iii
all afternoon and half the night;
swallowed phenobarbital,
listened to Elaane, her white knight:
'Darling, get *back* on that airplane,
dark London skies will drive you insane;
fly tomorrow; take my advice,
really you don't have much choice.
DO NOT ARGUE, fly to Sardinia.
Any emergency, via Rome
straight to Lebanon (closer than home).
M-skype Parker from Maddalena,
Eugenia has broadband, we know.
Remember skyping De Angelo

Twenty-ten? I was really smitten. iv
Only over in Capo d'Orso
with his wife, the bimbo kitten,
remember her?' Gala, very so-so,
drugged, manages a smile, falls asleep.
(From bedroom see Elaane creep.)
The decision is the right one;
the night rain is a light one
this evening. The river winks
its coloured eyelashes of traffic;
no stars or moon. (The topographic
map of the city has such brinks ...)
Under clear skies, the following night,
Laane drives Gala to her flight.

London too stays under sedation v
as sleeping Galatea wings south.
Soap operas for the population;
newscasters with the blabbermouth
telling everyone what to think.
The city's had enough to drink;
the bars are rammed with conscription teams.
The world's full of the Lebanon's screams.
'The British ambassador has quit
Damascus following allegations
which have put a strain on relations.'
And so on, all the usual Brit
understatement, innuendo, spin.
(Nothing like a war to wear truth thin.)

The nightraid on Al Qaryatayn, vi
was it the British, the Israelis,
MI6, Mossad's black campaign?
'Same thing,' scream Arab dailies.
'When Syria took the Golan Heights
she gave up international rights.'
Hawks drone; western talking heads
make their own hypocritical beds
to sleep in (dirty and soiled with lies)
writhe in crumpled double-standards;
while dark clouds of grand wizards
settle down like carrion flies
on the blown carcase of politics,
obscuring with *filthy* occult tricks.

On Maddalena with J and E vii
the first evening came M ringtones:
'M-channel calling, zone Twelve LB.'
(Parker's code for Lebanon phones.)
And in the twilight of the bedroom
both knew well she saw his face loom
out of the splashscreen. 'Gala'
he murmured. (She saw his pallor,
his left shoulder in broad white bandage.)
'Hello.' Propped up in bed with faint smile:
Parker, looking pale and fragile.
She could just detect foliage,
behind his head, a citrus tree,
maybe lemon; she tried to see

Into his eyes; they looked at his screen, viii
not at her. When she'd cried, he said:
'I escaped lightly, my love; it's been
ten times worse for Flynn, amputated.
This thing's skin-deep, I won't be here
in three weeks. Not till next year
will Big Ben even go prosthetic;
he's on sledgehammer anaesthetic.
(Nothing on the night went as planned,
can't explain.) But listen, I'm fine.
And glad you're in the Med sunshine.
Tell J and E your hell-bent husband
is on an archaeological trek
looking at the base of Baalbek.'

She half-smiled. (An in-joke.) Strange! ix
Remembered their age-old ambition
to study (under the mountain range)
Heliopolis of Lebanon.
'Have post-op given you thumbs up yet;
what says your specialist? I'm upset
you're not awarded home leave!'
Gala questioned, wanting to inweave
another topic, keen to commence
discussing psychotherapeutics,
all psychomedicine's new tricks.
(Exposure therapy *so* made sense.)
But she held back, heavy hearted,
listened to her husband; who started

Talking about night alerts. x
'Hizbollah's still hanging about;
but I'll tell you what really hurts:
not speaking to you when I doubt
myself in this situation.
Ben's injury; amputation:
could I have protected him more?'
Gala had been here before
many times, knew what to say;
felt false repeating the formula,
wheeling out the incunabular,
though she would have said it anyway:
'Darling, you're the bravest man on earth.
Don't ever, ever doubt your worth.'

She sensed his mind's movement looped: *xi*
memorized circles, trauma vortex.
Drugged, his eyelids slightly drooped:
shutdown of cerebral cortex.
'We're (yawn) near the Platform of Baalbek.'
Blip! (Transmission seemed to check;
the screen gave a small shudder:
just the subliminal persuader.)
'I'll see the Temple when I'm fixed.'
Gala shivered in the gloom,
felt a shadow presence loom.
Parker whispered: 'This war is jinxed '
Blip! He backtracked: 'Any good parties;
been to Madame O'Flaherty's?'

He changed tone after his gaffe, *xii*
mentioned their old town haunt;
managed to make Galatea laugh
referring to some old night jaunt
through Chelsea in student days,
(when they'd dreamed of different ways).
Antiquity had obsessed them both:
particularly the 'rapid growth'
civilizations; whose remnants
(most spectacularly Baalbek,
history's fortress, sacred wreck,
cyclopean mystery of romance)
seemed to speak of a golden age
dimly remembered on the page.

Written in gigantic letters xiii
here were transcripts from the past;
capitals of ancient typesetters,
initials from stone alphabets, vast,
(modernity couldn't work today).
Up in Baalbek's quarry lay
(single block of twelve-hundred tons)
the signature of the giant ones
who built here, quarried out an 'I'
from limestone time could not forget,
monolith that said: 'Remember yet,
and do not think I can ever die.'
Gala had the sudden grim
vision of an artificial limb …

A stone leg for a wounded Titan, xiv
a fallen angel called Ben Flynn.
She shivered inwardly, frightened;
vertiginous panic made her spin.
(Head and brain whirled suddenly.)
If only Parker had – if only
he'd – put faith in archaeology
alone. (She'd done anthropology.)
'No parties, but I've met the painter,
McCool. Most likely I'll interview
him, but he's more interested in you
than in …' Her voice grew fainter.
She saw that Parker was asleep.
Still connected she began to weep.

Late that night from Homer Gala read: *xv*
'Sit down here, please be seated.
Let's calm ourselves, put our griefs to bed,
so our heart's fires not be heated
again. We feel all pain's arrows:
only the gods live without sorrows.
Surely when misery and blessing
fall as equal gifts it's distressing
enough; but what about pure pain?
Some seem to go through life doubled
under endless curses, so troubled
when the gods send nothing but rain.'
Gala shut the book, tears streaming.
(Parker, far off, of her was dreaming.)

Sleepless near dawn she called Elaane, *xvi*
turned to her twin sister in distress:
'Lady Earth, can I please explain –
confess a little – I'm nothing less
than a fallen woman at this time,
an adventuress: it feels a crime.
I'll remain faithful to Parker;
yet I experience a darker
desire to give myself to …'
(Her sentence remained unfinished.)
'Darling, I feel so diminished.'
Sagely, Laane managed to segue
into a monologue less tragic.
(Up her sleeve she had some good magic.)

'Gal, I sympathize, understand, xvii
know exactly why you fled London.
Love is a kind of quicksand
sucking you down. Seeking the sun
was never your real incentive;
you were searching for a preventive.
(Anything to keep one safe
when desire's hot demons chafe.)
What a time for romance to strike.
You dream of entanglement with Tyg;
but you don't have to renege
on your marriage because you feel like
this – try to be more detached.
Anyway, you two are so mismatched,'

'Though contraries have their attraction. xviii
Water and air: multicoloured spray.
(Visionary art's chain-reaction
will encircle the earth one day.)
I sense you're scared of Tyg McCool.
His wildman makes you see the cruel
dragon that holds the world in its jaws,
(perhaps even some of Parker's flaws).
And now you fear for Parker's life.
What a panorama of hell
with heaven thrown in as well:
you're barefoot on the blade of a knife.
Gal, darling, I know you're not fickle.
You need a philosopher's circle.'

'Find a remote stretch of sand *xix*
later today. (Hey, it's meant to be!)
Four archangels are close at hand;
oracles do speak from the sea.
From a point (which becomes your centre)
trace a perimeter; and enter
conscious of the four directions.
In each of your mystic sections
place these: a candle for Parker,
Leo, to the south; water for you,
Gala, in the west; salt, your true
friend here, at the north marker;
in the east of air: sandalwood oil.
Then sit down on the sandy soil.'

'Face north. Be still an hour. *xx*
Let sea-washed Sardinian air,
scent of the magnolia flower,
blow through your flying hair.
Gal, shall I be very honest now?
I doubt you two will ever vow
(till the Sea of Milk runs dry,
till the sandgrains of personae
have run through the hands of God)
to love. Your man will really change
in the Chicoma mountain range
I predict. (That space age method,
psychotherapeutics, is our one
big hope when all's said and done.)'

'Meantime enjoy the sun of the south.' *xxi*
Laane pauses; Galatea's asleep.
Dark hair trails across her mouth,
smiling through two wisps. 'Sleep deep.
Somehow tonight you look windswept
like that Maddalena who has wept
in della Francesca, but who's free
because of the light she can see;
yet there's written across her face
the bittersweet confession of a past,
the woman of Venus before Christ,
sleepwalking on high cliffs of grace,
one stray strand hiding her full lips,
black hair flowing down to her hips.'

Gala, snoozing in pink pre-dawn, *xxii*
dreams she's dancing with a child
on the sand. (With her firstborn?
The son she's wanted so long?) Wild,
he moves in circles, cartwheels,
features finedrawn. Now she kneels,
catches him in her arms to kiss
his tiny fingers; feels fierce
love, wonder in her dreaming.
In this platinum moonlight
everything is certain to come right.
Ocean, in the background gleaming,
green waves pounding like a magic drum,
promises to her: elysium.

6 McCool tracked the phases of the moon, i
following the lunar goddess,
forever learning to attune
with that transient silver actress,
so as to ride – surf – her tides,
take advantage of her different sides.
When she was full he worked all night;
when she was dark and out of sight,
three or four days he would break,
look with retrospect at passion,
take perspectives of dispassion:
called this process: 'Staying awake.'
(First quarter: 'Discovery of strength.'
Tyg was on another wavelength.)

He felt supernaturally ii
extraphotosensitive, more light
making him, biochemically,
mentally, spiritually, ignite.
At full-moon a dimensional shift
gave his vision fantastic lift.
Polarized rays reflected back
across the planet woke the wolfpack,
intoxicating painters: light-drunk!
Then: the nightlong ruminations;
the sexual illuminations.
(McCool really wanted to debunk
the anti-romantic feminine:
women were magical within.)

On the cycling disc of la lune iii
he kept a kind of weather eye bent.
He was tracking the Drunken Moon
spinning through July at this moment,
the Hay Moon, reminder of backdays
trashed in arts-factory squats; green haze;
Thunder Moons rising across red-hot
horizons: nights of retrospect. What
dawns on the watchtowers of art!
The sun snorting a line of cocaine
from the horizon of Aquitaine
which sets him up, outside and apart.
(Tyg once said: 'When the sun sees his face
in the full moon's mirror: that is grace.')

Those were the days. Now, of late, iv
he did less drugs and more yoga;
nowadays he could discriminate
(he was much less of an ogre)
between worthless and permanent.
McCool was his own determinant.
Also his work's severest critic.
He never spared analytic
zeal, had no sentimental weakness
for executions second-rate,
for something he'd come to hate.
(But everywhere he saw uniqueness
where others saw nothing special.
The moon to him was beneficial.)

At the time (on a lunar yardstick) v
when McCool and Gala (by my will)
met, he was working in acrylic
on *Generation K* (at it still)
grotesque superimposition:
inner city and desert mission,
South Central Los Angeles
laid on top of a Middle East
battlezone; American concrete
merging with the alleys of Najaf.
In foreground, with hard-hitting laugh,
slick-spitting in a dry, dusty street,
a teenager seemed to dance on death:
a corpse made you want to hold your breath.

Outstretched in white djellaba, vi
Kalashnikov across the sand:
one dead rebel of the kasbah.
(Dude who'd had at his command
in English just the legendary
ten words of his flocabulary:
'represent', 'l train', 'show and prove',
'ghettobird', 'gangsta', and 'groove
weed' of course: the whole strength of it.
Who'd loved American street music,
the soul thaang, that outlaw mystique,
jazz, hiphop: the whole wavelength of it.
Who'd liked nothing else from the States,
none of what America dictates.)

Here was McCool's irony: vii
soul brothers of the battlegrounds,
through war's protracted agony
in eachother's faces firing rounds,
in war-stricken places 'dancing',
boots across skulls advancing.
(Trampling Rumi's bittersweet line:
'Torment of life can undermine,
bring down the giants of courage:
but *dance* sets the human spirit free.')
Well, I was among the first to see
Generation K – its afterimage
burns on – one of McCool's hottest,
one of his finest to be honest.

(Sold Stateside for eight million bucks viii
only three years later, c'est la vie;
if only those with deluxe
taste in art made foreign policy.)
Work on the canvas had stopped
the day my little trio dropped
over to De Beauvoir Town.
A dying moon was nearly down,
her bright fourteen had passed, vanished.
(Three dark days of non-projection,
then, eastward, lunar resurrection.)
Generation K was banished.
Maybe *Battlefield in Helmand*
was on the easel, the 'witness stand',

I don't remember, but do recall ix
about a fortnight afterward
getting a negative camcall
from McCool in a downward
morbid spiral of depression:
'A dead muse gives me the impression
my war-whore's fucked! *Generation K*'s
getting on my nerves today,
just wanna burn it.' On and on,
ad infinitum, like a wheel
turning on an automobile
racing downhill, three-quarters gone
out of control on a disastrous course
headed for the stone wall of remorse.

He'd been attemping to paint, x
reading from the Old Testament;
but first-quarter light, he felt, was faint.
He'd invoked the void of wonderment
(that vacant eye of the slavewoman
who waits – craves – to be awoken
by whom Pablo called 'the bull').
Yet spiritually he was still full,
from before, of that beauty,
when (quo vadis?) in late afternoon
(in the waxing of the Flower Moon)
Gala, *fierce*, not just tutti frutti
(looking like Sophia Loren
returned, exotic and foreign)

Appeared: tall, far-eastern queen, *xi*
unlaughing with her slanting eyes,
stern gaze of tilted almonds, green;
solemn in her glances, yet, surprise,
a trick of floating her head lightly,
making her aura flash brightly.
(Airs of a great lady, muted
presence of distant music, suited
to funerals, dirges for the year,
slow and stately, low and calm,
like some deep hypnotic charm
made Gala seem formal and severe.)
Tyg, himself such a contradiction,
fell beneath her dark benediction.

Now, in blue mood, surveyed canvas *xii*
(primed) with boredom, indifference.
Hadn't he manoeuvred, made a pass
at this madonna, talked sense,
maybe offered something absurd,
even transcendental? Not a word.
Her sandal'd played on the Kashan's nap
(running her instep, one silver strap)
angled on a blue-gold background.
(Elaane, outside, he'd heard laugh.)
A green lamé dress had more than half-
concealed bronze limbs; as she'd fooled around,
from her bare foot came a flash of light.
(Tyg Lorcan McCool checked out the sight.)

In white collar, with no cleavage, xiii
she seemed to wait for him to speak;
wore no makeup, looked her age
(thirty-something?) offered an oblique
half-smile of melancholic splendour.
He found words of the troubadour
Miraval, in love so discerning,
from distant memory returning,
revenant lines burning in his head:
'Lower your voice, raise your argument:
lover, you will need the paramount
subtlety to take this one to bed.'
(At that point Elaane had wafted through,
mentioning the painting up on view.)

We all saw Gala's impact on Tyg, xiv
man so contradictory.
(Armies of women laying siege
to his studio meant victory
for a side of him which didn't care:
he threw girls out in mid-affair.
Supersensitive to beauty,
McCool felt his perverse duty
to paint only the macabre;
would not deal with the graces,
could never suffer pretty faces
in his compositions sombre.)
Now the 'player' faced a different foe;
more than canvas to be set aglow.

Canvas stared back, insolent void, xv
nothingness, lightzone, testing ground.
Sight-blinding emptiness annoyed;
hot rays burned, made migraine pound.
Lancing brilliance, spear-thrusts of white,
photon bullets raced to smite
his retina, made him wince;
he shouted, squinted, went to rinse
tortured eyes with witchhazel,
juiced carrots and torch ginger,
acupressured with his finger,
lay with mask of refrigerant gel …
Nothing worked – zero relief –
he couldn't even think of a motif.

Gridlock, standstill. *Generation K?* xvi
Halfway finished. *Under the Gun?*
Stalemate, impasse, no possible way,
an abortion! Yet another one
awaiting his late muse, just deceased
(and some blowups from the Middle-East
sourced on the internet this time).
Number three – BITCH! – titled *War Crime* …
McCool gave a screech of panic
(climbed to his roofdeck, rolled a spliff),
gazed along the leaden reach as if
inspiration to end his manic
frustration lay in filthy tainted
slowly-drifting waters. He'd painted

The Grand Union, made sketches, xvii
thinking of his *Tigris Images*.
Now he stared at greenish stretches
pointing west: urban haemorrhages,
rectilinear anti-waterways,
ghosts of lost rivers of earlier days.
Flicker from stagnant water rayed
through narrowed eyelids played
a gold effect of dancing beams.
Random pathways of radiance,
scintillations of ambience,
hit optic nerves, made happenchance schemes
in a brain now much more relaxed.
(McCool's suddenly a lot less taxed.)

A droning sounds very high: xviii
a whirlybird, being used to drag
a black flag across cloudless sky.
('Internet gambling,' says this washrag,
'has never ever looked so good.')
McCool hears, ignores. It's understood:
'They're fishing in the city's cesspools,
searching for open-mouthed fools
who play math with probability,
dreaming "someone" (so to speak)
sometimes sends a winning streak
because of popularity
upstairs.' Remains in trance;
on water, dazzled, watches sundance.

The chopper fades to Islington; *xix*
Grand Union waters change.
Green shimmerings seem to bring on
(the Drunken Moon is coming) strange
altered states (that sort of half-sleep
where silent mind can make a leap).
McCool, in full lotus, sees *light*
(from blade of sunfire upright
on bright surface balanced) eerily
racing over incandescent space.
Sunrays, piercing shafts of grace,
fly. Wounded extraordinarily,
he feels – is – multipenetrated
by solar javelins goldplated;

Rolls onto his sunny roofdeck *xx*
transfixed; with slow sideways turn
takes a foetal posture; feels his neck,
where at the back it seems to burn
as if a chink in psychic chainmail
has let – enlightenment? – prevail.
Then, with miracle precision,
mysteriously, in field of vision,
a firewater forms, shaped round,
elongated above, downcurving
where his *paintbrush* goes swerving:
a rainbow falling with no sound
on the face, beside the water,
of the one called: *Scorpio's Daughter*.

Canalside, she stands alone, xxi
sad Renaissance madonna
in the rain, in twilight, *on her phone* …
(Dusk has descended on her.)
In the cosmology of her face
stars of interstellar space
flash and blaze from eyes storm-lashed;
as a single tear, with fiery splash,
falls from cheekbone's promontory:
in this one fragile sphere all the pain
deluged on earth in driving rain,
in experience fragmentary.
A face incarnates agony
and beauty: wild symphony.

Around sunset Tyg phoned Gala. xxii
She jumped onto Sardinian sands
(where she'd designed a mandala)
answering to her phone's demands,
saw his name, didn't select.
His message, replayed by the elect
two-horned Moon of Thunder coming,
started: 'Gala, hey, what's drumming?
McCool. What's good with you, what's new?
Something bizarre. If and when we link
I'll explain. Somehow in a sunblink
I saw today, in a glimpse (it's true)
you, in a painting. And I wondered …'
For Gala, wet, the crescent thundered.

7 Knightsbridge, something you lack i
strikes us from shopfront sun-mirror:
light, making a sudden attack,
its liberation getting nearer.
A perfumed emporium dazzles,
yet something in appearance puzzles.
What is this vacuity,
this glaring incongruity?
We're alienated here, glitter
blinds us at noon. (Confusion,
modern anxiety and delusion.)
This is why the world is bitter:
some have all and others none.
(There, my entire tale is done.)

The sun fumes like a diesel boat, ii
chugs along the blue skyzone;
clouds explode in a dry throat:
here is a sea goddess flown
in from the Sardinian Isles
only this morning, air-miles
shrinking, her bronze skin still wet.
She must drink soon (lag of jet).
Thus to the famous moated castle
which is where she'll meet Elaane:
it's Gala, just stepped off the plane
(still looking very coastal).
She's in the juice bar, island-fit:
fragrances drift, nu jazz, she's it.

A face from a dream of women. iii
She resembles the lady of El Cid,
eastern cheekbones, the cyclamen
with slanting wings; and there, amid
the flashing colours – a sense of flight –
her eyes are markings full of light,
with greenish rays, too exotic:
she is the deity aquatic.
Welcome ashore, divinity
only so slightly stressed, circadian
rhythms upside down, Arcadian
goddess of femininity.
She sucks at a gingered elixir.
Isn't that Elaane just over there?

'Gala, welcome back, my love.' iv
(As if she ever left, ah, never.)
'You look sea-washed, my white dove.'
(An understatement, as ever.)
Gala is in ivory layers,
pale sails on a skin which bares
golden secrets; and Elaane?
In this nautical refrain
she reappears, sweet bird of passage
drifting along horizons of time.
(Ages since this pair's initial rhyme
at the beginning of our voyage,
where line and aesthetic serve passion.)
Elaane is clad para-fashion:

Some jumpsuity military bits, v
kitten heels: absolutely ace.
Her smile's warm, genuine: 'It's
so *great* to see the one face
you've been really missing: Gala,
darling friend of the mandala,
I wanna know about the island,
hear news of your brave husband.'
Gala gazes down to the floor.
'He's mending fast, I think he's smoking;
I always know when Parker's toking:
let's not talk about the war.'
Laane: 'I know, it's serious,
half the army is delirious;'

'Think of firing a spaceage weapon vi
completely zonked.' Gala, she saw,
really did not want to reopen
the subject (discussed before).
They went on to a restaurant,
somewhere vegan and elegant,
visited some perfumeries,
late-afternoon galleries.
'In passing, here's a positive:
my interview with Baselitz,
the one where he finally admits
upside down is "not provocative
enough." Sometime late autumn
Apollo's printing it. A column,'

'That's what I really need from them; vii
and maybe the sungod's blessing.
Incidentally, someone (ahem)
wants to *paint* your confessing
nymphomaniac. (I plead guilty
to vivid fantasies which thrill me;
kill me too.) But I'm not a warzone!
(Or am I?) I have to be alone
because, unhappily, I'm married
to a man whose life is on the line.'
'Gala, honeychild, it's fine,
okay to get slightly carried-
away, be your own voyeur:
expectation's the destroyer.'

'Laane, you're cool.' 'No stresses, viii
he wants to paint you, that's a first!
Get your Cavalli dresses
out, be flattered, slinky, burst
with quotable, stunning Gala:
wartorn London is your La Scala.
We want to be at the private view,
on the top deck of what is new
in the cosmic imagination
if your face is the one to appear
"on the leylines", "in the air",
just when (at the last conflagration)
it seems the beautiful is banished,
gone, in the dark times vanished.'

'And guess what, babe? Valerie's barge ix
next Sunday night, on her riverboat:
Midsummer Moon! We'll have it large;
this weekend we'll have a river-float.
McCool will come (by a miracle)
that recluse.' (In this chronicle,
riding waves of vibrational thought
through a poet's mind in transport,
heroines of the transmission
to a cycle of stanzas turning,
they are in this endless burning
green maze by his volition:
racing through downtown at night,
their cab along the South Bank in flight.)

The river has its own career x
to follow, and these conform
to its excursions as they steer
through the city's emerald storm.
Gala sees reflections swaying;
seems to catch what the stars are saying.
(They streak across a bridge of light,
so anticipating Sunday night.)
Far off, a dot of contraction
slowly widens, a distant point
increasing. Will fate disappoint
those who begin an interaction
within her great circularity?
Will 'chance', by particularity,

Select two and make them one, *xi*
bring singleness where there were many?
Shall we see a new dimension?
(O multitude, have you not any
remote idea of your unity?)
Will love take this opportunity
to whisper something fragrant,
blowing off the sea with vagrant
messages from Aphrodite's crest,
raising up with crazy laughter
her waves of pleasure? And after,
when saltwater rolls back west
to ocean, will she say it again,
in race of foam over sandgrain?

Vauxhall, Gala's twin-deck. *xii*
Centuries ago she moved here
(bringing *Snakecharmer* from Purbeck,
and, of course, her vetiver)
in whose fronds a black flautist
hypnotizes, John the Baptist
androgyne of African rivers.
(His haunting lullaby shivers,
electrifies the human soul.)
Spirits of Niger and Zambesi
move on the Thames, free and easy
rhythm 'n' blues music of the whole
earth. This place is so transcultural:
a very cool town in general.)

Even in dark times, under dead moons, xiii
we need to peep through hot blinds,
see what the sun does afternoons
along the riverbank that winds
away into infinity.
A riverine divinity
has come to someone's rescue.
Excitement is nearby, right on cue.
(We won't – and don't – eavesdrop on a week's
telephonic cooings of this pair,
early flutings through digital air,
too girly, we have other techniques:
we'll just advance to the party!)
Through the usual glitterati:

Look, X and Y; they're an item. xiv
(Are we talking chromosomes?)
There are the Saatchis. (Must invite 'em.)
Among supercollectors, art-gnomes,
we recognize middle-aged rock stars
upstaged by taciturn gangstas.
In mists of Kali weed and chronic,
a pirate ship with electronic
atmospheres pulsating in the night,
all decks and levels, the Mindsweeper
(Val's summer salon) drifts deeper,
glides and shimmies out of sight,
riding an ocean of dub and zouk.
Metromusic, DJ Subjuke!

Up on the bridge, near the jacuzzi, *xv*
Val and her first mate, arm in arm;
near them, ah! here's Gala with Uzzi,
(high priest of metropolitan charm).
Over comes McCool, the painter
(others in the room look fainter).
'The new Picasso. Dude, all hail.'
(Uzzi's welcomes never fail.)
'My darling, meet Tyg McCool.
Ah, you know the man already.'
(With painted smile you seem unsteady,
Gala, but very Italian School,
Da Vinci to Modigliani:
the resemblance is uncanny.)

Galatea's suddenly steered *xvi*
into the whirl of a coloured tide;
here the carnival has veered
down a gangway, over the side?
(Dancers of the Mindsweeper
clearing the world of all cheaper
imitations of ecstasy:
body-linguists of fantasy.)
Out in the main crush, such a rush,
floating on the deep bassline;
stepping up to the divine
explosions of an airbrush
snare that splinters into echoes:
UK dub subculture! So it flows.

Elaane chugs past, poet in tow. xvii
How easily it is forgotten:
a long time since Gala let go,
free to dance in her delaine cotton
dress, hot soundsystem throbbing.
(Now the Mindsweeper's hull's bobbing
on a tropical sea of hiphop.
It's the pleasure zone, tip-top
deck.) And the Thunder Moon rallies
all dancers under her dominion,
quicksilver-full, milky companion
gliding through her cloudy valleys.
(McCool is in a mindless trance,
on autopilot, in a moondance.)

His, a face difficult to define, xviii
burned with a brand of wild years,
flames and flowers of the malign
from hard decades, dark frontiers:
the derries and the squat houses.
Every mark somehow arouses
respect for a veteran backstreet
man who endured through the nineties, heat
locked off in arts-factory winters,
one of the discombobulated
peeps (bubbles popped, evaporated)
their dialogues from Harold Pinter's
plays, painting through the Kings Cross nights,
trying to maintain the inner heights.

‘Aristocratic in the gutters, *xix*
damaged toff’: so McCool’s seen.
Gala’s green eyes hold his; Tyg utters
in cadenced drawl with Scots keen:
‘Och, okay, should’a worn the kilt.’
(Putting on the Caledonian lilt.)
The Drunken Moon (someone, support her)
is setting on Virginia Water;
she’s wandering, fortune wheel
spinning down into the west.
McCool and Galatea rest
forearms on the sternrail, feel
shy, fall silent. (They’ve been excessive:
the dancefloor stands for the transgressive.)

When he says: ‘Lift home?’ she’ll say: *xx*
‘I’m fine, I’m leaving with my friend
Laane who lives just over the way.’
(Liquid feminine tones blend
with the lapping of the tide
as high riverwaters glide.)
A silver ripple out there flashes,
an aquatic nightbird splashes.
Les Mystères des Voix Bulgares,
Ali Farka Touré, John Coltrane.
Music’s gone to the astral plane!
(Mountain-women, Malian guitar.)
On a smooth moonlit balustrade
two hands are almost overlaid.

Her lips *would* part under his mouth; *xxi*
to surrender her thoughts run.
(In consciousness she flies south;
the sweet hot tongue of the sun
sends his fire through her blood,
his kiss driving a solar flood
into her transfigured body.)
The river sings a rhapsody
to the moon, a cloudy song
full of laughing innuendo,
suggestive, with a crescendo
sexual. (Where are right and wrong?)
Gala, Venus in warpaint,
feels vaguely as if she might faint.

When his hand slides above hers, *xxii*
hers slightly retracts but must needs stay
positioned underneath. Now a bird's
multicoloured wings clap the Sunday
dawn full of Thunder Moon magic.
Listen – drumrolling angelic –
a heart flutters like a dove
startled while sleeping above,
beating in summer moonlight
from dovecot up to silvered roof.
Does Cupid need other proof?
(Someone sways in the sultry night.)
The marksman cherub's just released
a flight of hot arrows at his feast.

8 If time goes on slowing down i
the day won't be moving soon.
The hour hand is on strike; town
taps its foot to pollution's hot tune
lazily. Retarded by sorrow,
minutes drag toward tomorrow
reluctantly through mundane
dust. A corpse hangs, weathervane
on a towerblock stairwell, stinking
bell that tolls with sinister repeats.
Gang wars shuffle through the streets.
What can the Lord God be thinking?
Is He asleep? Does He have pity?
(Doomed love has done this to the city.)

Possibly yesterday's punishment ii
will not revisit the town; maybe
madness will return to some extent
tempered beyond the Red Sea.
Might sirens cease for one day,
allow music to have her say?
Could fountains perhaps reappear?
(They have been thought to be near.)
Might water play in the junction
(coast of skulls and closed circuit tv)
cool jets arise, a rosetree?
(Return: the river's social function
in the city. Raise the sacred Fleet,
fandango with citizens you meet ...)

That all seems doubtful; sedated iii
backstreets swelter. With no air
moving in this leadweighted
grey midday atmosphere,
no breeze is going to play,
no freshness can find a way
through London's slums and ghettos.
Sirens scream their falsettos.
Boredom of the underclass
erupts on the problem estates.
A single word – 'Lebanon' – stalemates
thought in a dustfilled underpass.
The only noonwind in this hell
carries bitter scent of shrapnel.

It's touched the sides of a pit iv
burning in eternity for men.
(Into that darkness all fit,
under destiny and its 'amen'.
Born into the separation
we make friends with annihilation,
threaten horizons with hellfire:
but go down in war's maya.)
London cooks in apocalyptic
microclimates of doomsday:
here's the horrific present-day
town as Last Judgment triptych
painted by some modern master,
entitled: *City of Disaster*.

Eastward Hackney is a shambles: v
this already destabilized zone
now economically gambles
on the help of Al Capone.
Flats drag on the sidewalk,
slap concrete like loose talk.
A woman walks through the ville;
she's trodden down her leather heel.
Catch her slurred speech when she offers
the best deal on her services
(under the brotherhood's auspices,
of course; half goes to Mafia coffers,
rest on the crack. Skeletons must smoke!
'A Sexworker's Guide to Freebase Coke':

Bestseller). Through garbage in the street vi
scattered, schoolgirls in facemasks
crocodile through stench bittersweet.
Marijuana dances bergamasques;
dreadlocked rustic mountain-rastas
shepherd the children, funky pastors.
Class attendance is nearly nil,
recruiting offices have their fill.
Icecream vans come out to play,
Red Riding Hood in pink lipstick
slinks along to *Teddy Bears' Picnic*.
(If you go down to the 'hood today
you'll hear the harsh bells of damnation,
decadence and war-desperation.)

Armageddon's brought booming trade vii
in girlflesh for the young material
hanging around the 'crusade
bars', where born again millennial
Christ-killing Christians hardsell you
anti-Islamic factsheets, tell you
the war is good in the sight of God.
(A streetgirl passes, sexily slipshod,
another blonde angel on the slide
as vice squad take their backhanders.)
Only fire-dwelling salamanders
can live out on the East side.
Do turtle doves still coo in this town;
any high romances going down?

We overlook and overhear viii
a camcall in the private domain
(connection, by the plot's engineer,
tapped between Vauxhall and Aquitaine)
a star-crossed lover's conversation
full of exquisite frustration,
subtle come-on, guarded display.
(Someone's feeling delicate today.
Actually, she's been a bit leaden
with persistent slight depression,
fallen after last month's jam session
when she was reckless. Gala, redden.
For Sunday night of the Mindsweeper
she's fond memories, feelings deeper.)

Our Lady of the Landline, prone ix
on sofa, calls wildman friend McCool
(who makes her feel less alone;
but distance is her golden rule).
'What fallen angels are you painting?'
'Well, there is someone … unrelenting.
But my battlequeen's taken flight:
dark dominatrix, she's a midnight
visitor to Aquitaine no more.
She's a stranger to my studio.
Either I'm burnt out, no libido,
or I'm finished with the Whore of War.'
'Neither's true I'm sure, O'Tyg'
(her nickname for him) 'you intrigue'

'More and more.' 'Gala, I'm not joking; x
zero brainwaves here, nothing yet.
If I do paint something provoking
I'll fly you to the hot-zone, let
you zoom in, I don't know, on *something*.'
(His playful smile has a softening
effect on his rugged jawline;
his profile: avian, aquiline.)
'You're teasing me, be more specific:
you're reworking a warscene,
a treatment, you really mean,
in the genre of the horrific.
You should go on with *War Crime*;
all your battlepieces are sublime.'

‘You torment and trouble, that’s true. *xi*
But one day men (and women) will see
the killing fields as you do:
revelations of intensity.
Maybe it could change human hearts,
compassion that your work imparts.’
(Hiatus.) ‘Who knows? I’ve a plan,
vague, to return to Afghanistan,
to immerse in warzones, airstrikes,
massacres again; I need whirlwind
inspiration, nightmare of the kind
found near the Sulaymaniyah lakes
last year, for *Virgin of the Crane*,
my teenager hanging in night-rain.’

(McCool’s not *still* trying to co-opt *xii*
Gala into sitting for him?
No, that subject’s apparently dropped.
The truth is: he paints his seraphim,
a non-winged angel in this case,
portrays in heightened ways the face
memorized that Sunday night
HMS Mindsweeper took flight.
Now, in nocturne, he delineates
two sea-green eyes of saddened gaze;
suddenly in future noons they blaze;
at times a reluctant smile translates
into rainswept abstract stylised.
Has a demon muse supervised?)

(A magnum opus now begins. xiii
Like an alchemist who labours
with transmutations and toxins
out of sight of his neighbours
through small hours McCool slaves,
playing with colour and lightwaves
till the dawnpoints of sunrise.
Obsession's come as a surprise:
his burning to render this woman.
Never in his oeuvre since age nineteen
have high curvilinear cheekbones been
seen haunting masterpieces solemn.
Then he'd suffered semi-breakdown:
firstlove went into fiery meltdown.)

Our midnight painter doesn't mention xiv
to Galatea that possibly
she's been captured; his intention,
when she's *caught*, to let her see,
not some half-coherent likeness
but her true self-image: timeless.
And probably he manipulates,
as people do, in their loves and hates
(or is he absolutely sincere?)
when he adds: 'I need to return,
make another Mideastern sojourn.
Medécins sans Frontières
can smuggle me into Damascus.
But they say it's well-dangerous.'

‘Speaking of danger, Parker’s making *xv*
progress I hear.’ (Listen, from Vauxhall,
those tormented songs of leavetaking:
the *Kindertotenlieder*: ‘Looks all
sunny, my darlings, you seemed to say
here with me you desired to stay.’)
Gala, from Chesterfield (all’s revealed
from lips that have been tight sealed:)
‘My God – McCool – please don’t sacrifice
yourself. You’ve suffered for your art;
there’s sufficient hellfire in your heart;
you’ve already paid the highest price:
PAINT,’ she whispers in desperation.
‘CAN’T,’ he answers with resignation.

(The monosyllabic half-lie *xvi*
camouflaged with melancholy smile.)
Through night-window neon sky
flashes. Square mile by square mile
he scans surrounding city:
wasteland London, no pretty
lights, blurred nocturnal vistas,
only a raw wound with blisters
breaking open, all weeping
suppurating matter, seepage,
floods of psychological sewage,
discharge of an eversleeping
subliminal mass-psyche poisoned
by reveries of war unreasoned.

In a flash, like something freeing *xvii*
in his chest, his spirits seem to lift.
(Look, he surrenders in his being;
in his heart God's giving him a gift.)
'That's only half-true, I've been trying.
Gala, no more lies, let's go flying;
turn up Mahler on your radio.
Let's take off for my studio!'
He picks up his silver Airbook
(her screen swings wildly to and fro
though his movements – mobilizing – flow),
the same ultralight machine he took
east last year, when a mournful man
dragged himself through wartorn Iran.

Someone stands beside a river *xviii*
under a Modigliani Moon.
(Dawn suns rise, as if forever
in maiden flight towards noon.)
There is something in this face
familiar across time and space.
(Is it her, in filtered daylight,
where in a radiant twilight
all's shifted to the futuristic?)
Familiar, too, this streamlined
metropolis of intertwined
canals, rivers: surrealistic
(reminding us of sci-fi Turner).
Who's the postmodern Magdalena

Gazing from this atmospheric place, *xix*
dark bliss of the Snakecharmer
in the expression of her face
(what could possibly harm her?),
yet sad, as if (in the foreground)
one whom the riverzones surround
is not fully present in the flesh,
dreaming only, a way to refresh
herself with forbidden caprice.
(A long phrase of stately metre
in the *Kindertotenlieder*
slowly resolves and finds release.
Mahler's dark songcycle ends:
cadence to conclusion descends.)

Gala's confused by these delights; *xx*
this sci-fi city of future days
full of incomprehensible sights:
flumes, translucent waterways,
blue cubed sky-pools and sky-rivers
snaking through tropospheres; divers
plunging from high transparent tanks
(stepped through cloudbase in blue ranks)
down some *new* metropolitan sky.
(See! They crash, flocks of swimmers
breaking aquamarine that shimmers;
these skydancers who pretend to fly.
Splash! Another flock – or is that fleet? –
landing in the oceans at her feet.)

Her own image (poetic reader, *xxi*
you understand) brings bewilderment.
Attracted and repelled like Leda,
her response is ambivalent.
(Love pushes her, love pulls her back.)
She's surprised by sudden attack,
recoils in pain, returns for more,
flees from love's still-wilder shore.
Yet this is not procrastination:
if he loves darkness, she needs joy.
Gala's no tease; she's not being coy
or playing with anticipation:
her devils are duty and deceit.
(His demons lie down beneath her feet.)

Pleasure gardens of excellence. *xxii*
(Do we believe in them?) Say something,
Galatea; qu'est-ce que tu penses,
Gala? Are you love's plaything,
arrayed now as McCool sees you
in watercities of his brave new
world? You still seem interior
somehow, removed from (superior
to) these citadels of stained glass
with marine streets, blue cataracts
holding mysteries as spray diffracts
metallic rainbows on crowds who pass.
Lifted above millions, self-possessed,
you stand on a multicoloured crest.

9 Waiting for the sun to descend i
(shadows, after noon's focus
slid on hot stone, started to extend)
Parker in the Gate of Bacchus
watched a gunship roar down-valley,
from blue markings: Israeli.
Across the sunburned dreamscape
he saw a blur of human shape
moving through the heat-bent air,
traversing the acropolis,
the courtyard of Heliopolis.
A fighting man was in despair.
(Shifting in dimness of the gate
Parker felt left-trapezius grate.)

Medically he was improving; ii
inwardly he was in turmoil.
With shoulder mending, no removing
of bone (the dry air seemed to boil),
his agony was for Ben Flynn,
nearer to him than his own kin.
Suffering too Balkan flashbacks,
new hallucinations brought Pec's
ancient nightmare to life: death
hunting Patrick, smashing his skull
with sudden, matter-of-fact, dull
sound of impact, one last breath
blowing from the body mixed with brains.
Parker lived in recollection's chains.

‘Don’t ever, *ever* doubt your worth.’ iii
He returned to his hospital bed,
revisited a Baalbek sickberth
where he’d been lying when Gala’d said
those sincere words. (Often repeated
down the years – beside him seated,
his wife – her generous nature
lessening long-drawn-out torture.
Always if he’d woken screaming
in the past, his redeeming angel’s
fingers had cooled inflamed temples
when heat of the bad dreaming
had left him, fevered, half-insane
after midnight. Fires of Beltane!)

Dark. Under night’s dim ceiling. iv
Advance! Men on hands and knees
in a minefield. Nauseous feeling;
stomach tense. Then, from trees,
rocket-propelled grenades streaking:
one evil dart of hot steel seeking
the head – the face – of his friend:
destroying-angel of the end,
ripping flesh, tearing skull apart
from trunk, leaving torso headless
swaying fountain, red and helpless
bleeding tower with human heart.
(Pat’s face gone, nothing remaining.)
Once, after the Balkans, regaining

Consciousness, she'd said: 'Relax, v
think of that miracle in Homer:
laughter of the child, Astyanax.'
(Her voice penetrating his coma.)
Even now her words could wake him
when dark memories would take him
to Tartarus from wartorn Baalbek.
(A bloodsoaked regimental roll-neck
sweater surrounding what was left:
the spinal column still sticking out;
scorched wool-nylon tricking-out
Pat's naked backbone, neck-cleft,
burning stench on the night air sharp.)
A soldier hears the sound of a harp:

Voice of a slowly spinning dove vi
in the Gate of Bacchus: soothing,
tender crooning, keening above,
(troubadour-song, peace-approving,
ardent, against the stridors of war)
chant of that tranquillity before
when they'd been lovers on a beach
at twilight, 'far from the twisted reach
of crazy sorrow', as someone said;
living not for remote phantom
tomorrows, calculate per annum.
(Eyes closed against the sun, in his head,
he sees her slanted gaze – a dove sings –
there are white fantasias of wings.)

The burning day had lost its gloss vii
when, semi-blind, he squinted out
from solemn shadow. Total loss,
ruin of everything, tinted out
colour: black-and-white world!
A tear stood as a dove twirled
in the gate above and behind.
Darkness raced into his mind.
He imagined Galatea *false*,
saw her dancing with a stranger;
felt his sanity in danger,
a jealous heart seemed to convulse.
He took two more Zoloft to remain …
Nerves in left shoulder tugged again.

A single transport helicopter viii
thundered through late Baalbek
stillness, hovered like a raptor
over the hospital, bridgedeck
flashing, matt-black whirlybird.
A medic-team abseiled downward:
fresh blood. The soldier visualized
life sucked from men devitalized,
a mechanized vampiric insect
extracting bitterness of death,
not sweetness from a flower's breath.
(Parker's overdoses took effect:
hallucinations of the drug.)
Westward droned the flying bedbug.

The dusk air, violently juddered, *ix*
slowly grew calm. In deep blue
twilight Col. James shuddered,
from inner pocket withdrew
his black pen. (A sculpted poppy
deep in stone was a carbon copy.)
The colonel knew where he was going;
pressed down until ink was flowing
dark onto his old notebook's
righthand page; then began:
'Darling Galatea, here's your man
writing to you from strange outlooks.'
(A wild drunken Lord of Excess
watched, laughing, from a carved recess.)

'I trust your painter, that trendsetter, *x*
is behaving better. Your tension,
frustration, showed in your last letter;
where, near the start, you mention
exposure therapy. Sounds cool!
Sit in a dome and play the fool
in the sun in New Mexico.
This coming November, let's go!
Look, I'm plunging in the deep end,
but I'm for real, I'm serious.
There is something mysterious,
destructive, in my state of mind;
I admit I'm ill; I need help:
my brain feels beaten to a pulp.'

'This letter's difficult to write *xi*
'coz I'm so high on medication:
new drugs every week – I'm a bombsite –
Cycloserine, Seroquell, Station;
the antipsychotic Depakote,
Catapres, the madness antidote.
Some are hallucinogenic,
rumours say, mutagenic,
scary stuff. Back to the point:
I've been army through and through,
now I can't analyse what or who
I am; my pride's at breakpoint.
A leader of men on his knees,
a warrior saying "Pretty, please"?'

'I'm finished! My mind's in smithereens; *xii*
it's quit-time. We'll have to sell the house.
Resigning my commission means
we'll lose a lot of income, because
(you understand, of course, the answer:
the Queen pays well her loyal Lancer).
We'll miss Rain Hill, I know we will,
but we can plan to have children still.
(They'd have loved those Purbeck meadows.)
We'll move back to tired old Chelsea,
a small townhouse, nothing too fancy
(as I reenter Academe's groves).
If peace comes in the Great Rift Valley
perhaps we'll excavate here freely'

‘One day, you and I, penetrate xiii
the dark foundations of Cain,
decipher this grandeur’s great
secret, enter the arcane
world of the antediluvians,
find ruins beneath the ruins,
stumble on sleeping bones of men
who lived before the Flood (when
giants – extraterrestrial? –
walked the earth, in the Bible
such a fascinating fable
from aeons immemorial).
My Sufi contact Abdul Kad’r
mentions often old tunnels here;’

‘I feel this is the way ahead. xiv
I’ve dreamed about a stone door,
a passageway to realms of the dead
snaking down through subterranean core
deep into cyclopean levels.
People say Nephilim devils
still live far beneath the temple
(on the surface we’re an example)
underground generations of Cain
metalworking beneath the “jebel”:
the killer of his brother Abel
hiding from the eye of God in vain.
(The drugs – I’m rambling – it’s the pills.)
I know I’m tilting at windmills,’

‘But this war’s doomed; I don’t believe xv
peace can come from hatred’s harvest;
we play tricks on ourselves, self-deceive.
The reason we’re in the Middle East:
to keep the Western engine running.
Oil, not democracy: rat cunning!
The planet burns one hundred tankers
per day; our international bankers
make absolutely sure crude’s sailing
daily out through the Scorpion’s Gate,
the Straits of Hormuz, where of late
an atmosphere’s been prevailing:
American and Chinese flatdecks
sizing up eachother’s nuclear specs.’

‘Deployment, I wanted to like you, xvi
imagined you’d help me to forget
the worst a man can go through,
losing his friend from one cigarette
to the next; but, deployment,
you led me by evil decoyment
to where the pain was more intense,
darkness of the curse more dense,
to where I feel I’ll lose my wife,
the woman I want, the one I love.
Gal, I fear this, my faraway dove,
more than the loss of my own life.
Last night (imagine, darling) I dreamed;
about that summer when all seemed’

‘In the garden of Gloucestershire, xvii
beneath a towering sycamore
(remember when young love caught fire
beneath that godlike tree?) evermore
perfect. We first smoked marijuana
that night; knew the brief nirvana
delivered by the psychoactive,
felt we’d only then begun to live.
I found my manhood in your arms;
we kissed with shy but eager tongues
(sunlight exploding in our lungs).
Spinning in aphrodisiac storms
naively we learned to love,
whirlwinding in a dance high above.’

‘That carnal night beside the river xviii
winding down from Guiting Power,
when the water seemed to deliver
flesh to its immortal hour.
Soft sounds of liquid lapping;
on riverbank, slipping-slapping;
nightcallings of a secret blackbird.
(From silent heart a whispered word.)
Sunday dawned, we found a church
across a lake, above the Windrush,
southward over valley floor lush:
Saint Mary’s. And so began my search.
Since there first I saw that fatal wheel,
wooden, on the wall: the Templar seal.’

‘Like a serpent coiled in the Sunday *xix*
silence of the Cotswold hills,
in that paradise of honey-
coloured villages with windowsills
innocently flowered, my destiny
lay in wait for me: the military.
(Later your gypsy friend assured –
Tanya – I’d been a feudal lord
invading the Mediterranean,
carrying a crimson Templar cross
on my chest, in dusty chaos
of medieval centuries when
men rode to rewin Jerusalem,
proud of that blood-red emblem.)’

‘She said: “I see a suntanned face.” *xx*
(My own features superimposed
on a man of different time and place.)
We doubted her airy stuff disclosed,
but now, look, I’m a crusader,
in old Outremer an invader.
(Tanya, I recall, tried to explain
sadness of a distant chatelaine
as she gazed back to previous days.
She looked at a coloured playing card,
said to me the words: “Dieu vous garde.”)
She saw the past through a haze,
all was brushed by an angel’s wing,
then she wasn’t sure of anything.’

'I send you a thousand kisses, hugs, xxi
just for now put this letter on hold;
here in the gate of the God of Drugs
I'm gonna smoke some Lebanese Gold.
All these chemicals keeping me calm
don't compare with this little balm.
Here's a solemn promise, remember:
we'll go Stateside in November!
I'll resume tomorrow without fail.
Right now I'll walk up to the quarry;
the sun's just disappeared in glory
with a multicoloured twilight trail
behind the Lebanon range sinking.'
The colonel moved slowly, thinking.

Parker stood by the megalith xxii
broad as a house, long as a street.
Dwarfed by the Stone of the South,
emotionally bittersweet
he felt a Titanic arrow
piercing him with world-sorrow.
Flynn would never run again
across wild Enniskillen terrain.
He had no son. Gala was alone
in London of the temptations,
city of eternal flirtations.
He placed two hands on the warm stone,
smiled, and thought: 'If this was a spliff,
the world could be transformed in a jiff.'

10

And it is. But these aren't halcyon days i
from some golden noon of legend;
we plunge back into big-city haze:
London. No one can pretend
this is the Age of Aquarius;
where are those multifarious
waterways of the Waterbearer,
riverboats of a future era,
Mindsweepers of fullerene glass?
Where are dancers of transculture,
riverzones of blue curvature?
(All that may yet come to pass;
in the meantime make do with this:
Klingsor's photochemical abyss.)

We're at a party in Kensington, ii
in the upper entrails of the town.
(We envy that urban citizen
whose home is not in rundown
Catford, or sleazy Leytonstone.
Here, at least, an air of new-mown
gardens and green private squares
compensates local millionaires
for having to be around at all,
when they could be breathing deep
the fresh, clean winds that sweep
the Gower Peninsula.) A pall,
a shroud of diesel particulate,
reeks in London's microclimate.

We circulate, champagne glass in hand, iii
bored to tears, dreaming of escape,
through noise of tittle-tattle land,
where shrill voices howl and scrape,
where exercise of vocal chords
without much to say affords
the chatterati a fine chance
to evanesce in the social dance.
Here's someone quoting tabloid
revelations: 'Pilots on "go-pills",
the dexedrine that drives up the kills.'
One (more intelligent) factoid
amid hot air about distresses
caused by two-timing mistresses.

Meet Fran, knockout deb, nothing on; iv
her boyfriend does hedge funds, equity,
investment's his life (and badminton).
Divestment's her speciality.
Dancefloors are under discussion,
Goa, Ibiza, sea-percussion,
surf-whispers, romance in the haze:
beachparties versus urban days.
Like all angels, Fran is half-wave,
only just formed out of wild surge;
she feels her calling to submerge
in horizontal pleasures, a slave
to waters of choice destinations
around the world: perfect locations.

Here's Skye: it-girl, aquafeminist; v
jet travel's her religion.
(Tolstoy called her a materialist.)
On white coasts she's a cultigen
flowering out of the hot sand,
sea-green two-piece on suntanned
body: her dicotyledons,
eternal florescence of Edens
where beauty – she is of course
a prime example – luxuriates.
Only a few things she hates:
an ill-bred man on a fine horse
(any kind of patriarchal bore)
a landlocked country without a shore.

Background music's cheap pop mess: vi
if it wasn't so in-your-face
this cacophonic crowd might shout less.
Our ears, with serviettes in place,
dream of the garden. O, there's Gala
James, leaning on that painter fella
McCool: amazing supernova.
Conversation there will turn over!
But we can't escape the crowd,
claustrophobic, seething, jabber-mad.
Crones who shouldn't be scantily clad,
goons who have only one mode: 'LOUD,'
distract, interrupt, seize one's arm;
drag one off through the funny farm.

Which moon is this? Moon of the Dog. vii
What dog is that? The one who bays
when Isis peers through August fog,
low in the late summer days.
Our presumptive lovers have fled.
At a time when others are in bed
they haunt the town, talk in bars
far above red rivers of cars;
from a parapet of the city
look down through a luminous night,
an iridescent canyon of light,
an abyss of electricity.
Catch them at four in the morning
(the hour itself a danger warning).

They're in a lowlit corner, these two. viii
(On the surface all seems normal:
two sweethearts drinking, couples do
hang out in small hours, less formal
somehow, more intimate than early
evening when noise and hurlyburly
make it hard sometimes to be heard
if you need to say a special word.)
Yet these don't speak; or hardly at all:
he stares away across Hyde Park,
gazing at some inner landmark.
Perhaps marital deadzone, fall
from grace, end of a long road:
marriage as emotion-overload?

Gala's eyes are closed as if to say ix
the eve of destruction has come.
(Entanglement and breaking away:
the double beat of love's drum.)
She hears those trumpets of the end
which even love cannot transcend
in the Armageddon of the heart
(when Eros sends a poison dart).
Now she glances at McCool: lean-jawed,
taciturn, tortured, still unbeaten;
his air of proud decadence eaten,
marked by fire. She's overawed.
Wanting and desiring this man
she casts back to how it all began.

She'd seen a shot of *Hero Carcase* x
in swish Apollo magazine,
scanned it, lost it (without trace
somewhere in a hundred-and-nineteen
removable drives). His masterpiece
stayed with her, dark altarpiece,
its pathos of the dead man prone,
left for nightwind to bury alone
with a dry howl in the desert sand,
for jackals to dig under the moon;
for a soul to moan on a night-dune
somewhere in the province of Helmand.
Then, from database, as if willed,
the scan turned up when Pat was killed.

She was twenty-five: still dreaming. *xi*
(Parker'd sworn to try for a baby
before he left on a screaming
military jet for the maybe
'overexcited' Balkans.)
They'd talked about the suntans
they'd get in the Balearics;
before a rising of the Styx
washed up many forbidden things,
smashed skulls, deliriums, a red cross
which seemed to stand for a friend's loss,
a sea full of broken wedding rings.
(It made a fool's hope of all her faith,
that Globemaster fading like a wraith.)

Crying into a Snow Job, *xii*
she tells McCool the whole story,
takes a sip (as a crushed sob
is kept in) sweet cinnamon's glory
tingeing the white drink, full of tears.
And Gala has more unspoken fears
ice-cold upon her woman's heart.
(What a hope, mere words to impart
the secret feelings of another's soul.)
McCool tastes his Black Russian.
Is he still part of this discussion,
this one silent as the North Pole?
He takes her hand but looks away
across the darkness: nothing to say?

Six. In palace-garden they talk xiii
before the city starts humming;
by the Serpentine, on the Broadwalk,
through summer dawn see them coming.
At sunup, by walled garden's lake,
she feels like water the fountains take,
play with, throw down in disarray,
lift glittering into a new day,
only to dash to oblivion.
Will she ride a taxi on her own,
heart inside as heavy as stone;
or remain here in this elysian
early-morning with McCool?
And what about her golden rule?

A flight of swans comes in to land xiv
on the dazzle of the dawn lake.
Mute, these two, hand grazing hand,
watch the majestic birds make
touchdown on the water-mirror,
wide wings reflecting, nearer,
nearer, till skis tramline the surface;
and the white flock with eerie grace
thunders down the soft runway,
rippling silver, making shimmers,
spray of a million golden glimmers.
Tyg, on one knee on the pathway,
takes Gala's slender hand to his lips;
his cheeks brush her red fingertips.

His rapture burns hopelessly. xv
She is not free, nor can she relent;
his fruit from love's hanging-tree:
a dream of the impermanent.
Yet love proves what can remain
true in the face of time's disdain.
As she explores infidelity
he exploits a new fragility;
and runs his lips along her wrist.
(They're within the riverzones;
sunrise lights her milky skintones.)
Through jade and peach she has been kissed.
(It shouldn't be like this, of course;
but no one can resist magnetic force.)

A white swan flies toward them, xvi
wingspan wide, hovering cloud;
the goddess wears a sun-diadem
on her rapid glidepath, her proud
flight: her solar crown flares vast.
Far out in front, her neck's a mast
like the bowsprit of a brigantine,
wild beauty, something only seen
through a veil of coloured spray.
SSSSHHH: a diamond-studded welcome
from the water (sadly seldom
noticed, but here, now, anyway).
Ripples scatter from the landing: bright
waves goldplated with sunlight.

He still wants his vapid freedom; *xvii*
she regrets forgotten loyalty.
(If only the natural kingdom,
the swans in their royalty,
lay closer to the human world.
Look! In a tent of feathers furled,
within a pale canopy of cloud,
tiny cygnets ride a ship more proud
than any built with ribs of steel:
a vessel made of pure ivory.)
Gala kneels down by the golden sea;
it's so terrible a thing … to feel.
Her green eyes are misted by the shore;
she looks as he painted her before.

(Life imitates art, paintbrush splashing; *xviii*
here's a work immense yet intimate.
Let's have some more spangled flashing!
Shall we make the charged air vibrate?)
A ship of alabaster glides;
within her plumed sundeck hides
a trinity of newborn birds
sailing with her heavenwards.
(Here's the immaculate Signora
crossing the serene cosmos
out of night's serpentine chaos,
through a vast blue-gold aurora,
carrying her sunchildren – a sight! –
transporting them safe into the light.)

‘I’m terrified.’ (A speaking statue?) *xix*
‘There’s danger in the world of dreams.’
(Exactly who is talking to who?)
‘Nothing here is what it seems;
other dimensions interface
with this wartorn, suffering place.’
(With good reason to be separate
they stand close in their tete-a-tete.)
‘I prefer an angel to scare me
than a demon to bore me to death
with some comfortable shibboleth.
And you just *elsewhere* me.’
She inches closer to McCool,
in love’s shrine of light another fool.

My Gala, fierce and sentimental, *xx*
you’re so very contradictory.
(Maybe it’s only experimental;
quick, say something valedictory.)
An early walker in the park
sees two lovers near the watermark,
heads bowed like Adam and Eve,
without carnal knowledge so naïve.
(Can nothing for these two be done?)
God looks down on the Round Pond,
moves His rod of fire, His magic wand:
and they become mysteriously one,
four hands clasped, as a rain of tears
keeps falling in a garden of cares.

Shall there be special dispensation? xxi
Do you believe in a miracle,
what about transubstantiation?
Shall we have something quite lyrical
to close this chapter of events?
If love really represents
that highest force which drives the stars
we cannot put love behind bars;
no trite taxicab must bear away
our star-crossed lovers through the town:
we insist, because of love's renown.
A supernatural act comes into play.
(Get ready for the supramundane;
the sky is going to open over London.)

Into Klingsor's Garden of the west xxii
(where a princess has been confined)
falls a ray (which always shines its best
every time true hearts are intertwined).
All's shadow compared with this light.
(Our characters have walked in night.)
Here are: the winged car of creation,
the firebird of imagination.
Wheels within wheels, wings within wings,
our paramours pass a skyscraper,
glissade on expressways of vapour.
They're going to the watercity's rings:
flight of days – glimpse of the Snakecharmer –
gone! What an ending to this drama.

11 For God, His mirrorlike creation; i
for painters a half-nude pussycat.
She is *the* great meditation
for a true artist-ocrat.
That sweet taste of muscadel,
a seminaked model,
not much talking, time flying:
she, so happy, stretched out, lying
half-undressed beneath a gaze
obsessively trained only on her,
fiddling with some strap: Queen Poseur:
Miss Laze in an ataractic daze.
(The Absolute, on the odd afternoon,
likes to see the bright phase of la lune.)

But who's *this* model (in Aquitaine, ii
under the Corn Moon of the harvest)
raven-haired, almond-eyed, champagne
glass slightly tilted, self-possessed?
She's not sprawled in fishnet stocking;
she's not one of those shocking
half-naked angels of the kind
best appreciated from behind.
Gala looks down her tiffany mesh,
her sea-grey bodice under blue net,
its cotton of 'No one's been here yet',
sweet web that catches man-flesh.
Her dark hair trails toxic smoke.
(McCool gets her, brushstroke by brushstroke.)

Painters have gone very straight. iii
(Where's the conceptual Madonna?
The ashcan Mona Lisa's lost weight.)
This Eve: more curve and halo on *her*.
Tyg works like a man on go-pills –
Mo'drugliani nights – gone, his ills.
A Harvest Moon lengthens his rites.
He finds the ratio that delights,
the golden section in her face,
into the small hours painting
like a maniac. Gala's fainting,
she's drunk too much Aerospace.
(That's that new biotech caffeine
ginseng root spliced with coffee bean.)

(They said they would feed the world; iv
they put in charge a mental case
in a labsuit: and famine unfurled
its black flag for the human race.)
His world is such a warm one,
it's so sensual under his sun;
she loves to lie here basking in his air
of hardly noticing she's there,
yet almost completely obsessed
by the angle of her shoulder
(so that she seems meeker or bolder),
by what she does and how she's dressed.
(Gala looks sort of Russian tonight,
broad belt; high suede boots; bracelet: white.

She's in dark blue, velvet and leather; v
she looks Mediterranean too,
mouth slightly open: lightweight feather
fallen on a windowsill.) Debut
or practised posture? We don't know.
Is it an act, or has she let go
purgatorial formalities,
principles, moralities?
(She looks sad, as if she's been lonely;
melancholic, and that pleases him;
her atmosphere eases him.
Near her, he is no more only
himself but part of the beautiful;
focussed no more on the pitiful.)

Yet (what's happened?) is this still Crackney? vi
(Long, long ago in legendary
times there *did* exist a Cockney
earth-paradise (imaginary?)
with the evocative name 'Cockaigne'.
We haven't much time to explain
Atlantean myths of that city,
its multidimensionality.
I'd recommend Lewis Spence,
he's the man to proclaim
where the Cockneys get their name.)
Have we abandoned commonsense,
passed a fork in the river of time,
discovered another paradigm?

Anything's possible these days. vii
While art wants to be functional,
quantum mechanics is ablaze
with the frankly fictional.
If we like we can traverse
the ten-dimensioned multiverse,
with one more dimension for luck,
the eleventh, in which, dumbstruck,
we watch ultimate sturm und drang
insanity, see collide
two realities side by side:
explanation of the Big Bang.
Two universes in collision
on the eleventh plane: a vision?

No, this is the mystical stuff viii
the quantum poets bring to bear.
(The ear cannot get enough.)
Whirlpools of time, curvilinear.
Forget about particle and wave,
that old duality's in the grave:
wake up to fantastic superstrings.
A music of the spheres which rings
not *as* Pythagoras predicted
(nor precisely as Dante explained)
but near-as-dammit. If you've trained
your ear on skies *unrestricted*
you'll hear the audible lifestream.
It's the real deal: God's love theme.

So let's enjoy the flowermaiden, *ix*
the timewarp and the wormhole;
it's Hackney, but it's Arcadian
at the same time. Let's take a stroll
through a mindscape visionary,
underneath this luminary
urban moon which endlessly slants
her moonbeams, generously grants
more light than ever before,
this Barley Moon, night traveller
(this spacetime-fabric-unraveller)
freewheeling as in the days of yore,
futuristic as a world of platinum
crossed with rivers of molybdenum.

Time is suspended. Hypnotic sound, *x*
a waterfall distantly tinkles,
a prayerwheel going round.
Sirius by Orion twinkles.
McCool works like the god of making,
giving life to an awaking
world of form and multicolour.
His widespread angel (it is Gala
lounging back in starlit corona)
whispers (like surf in pleasure crashing
against the land that loves the lashing)
breathes: 'McCool ...' (Speak, sea-madonna.)
'Some might call me meretricious
but to relax is so delicious!'

He doesn't hear, it's been ignored. *xi*
And Gala's unrecognizable,
to herself she's been restored.
(Her dream's become realizable.)
A forbidden fruit has ripened,
a sunflower of light's opened.
She never senses time's flow
slaving for the maestro
McCool of the impassive gaze,
glance which distantly assesses her,
intimately possesses her,
passing through her nights and days,
transfixing her as in a myth:
angel with the name Lilith.

She lives in the third person *xii*
though the centre of attention.
(Is this some masochistic prison,
some psychodrama of detention?
Has identity been destroyed,
released?) Tonight she will not avoid
the deeper question: Who am I?
Gazing back into her own eye,
she'll see herself from over there
from that mythological land
where all is still and all is grand:
pictures painted by the god of air.
(Nine or ten more in the place,
all showing one enigmatic face,

Beautiful yet sombre and wild.) xiii
See the end of innocence portrayed,
the mark of the runaway child
in that mouth, where the eyes fade
to sadness and a fugitive
expression. You can forgive
this woman anything, she's pure.
(When does a portrait open a door
to Otherness? When you remember
who you are as you behold yourself
rendered by the master *himself*.)
Her beauty is a sleeping ember
one day soon to be blown skyhigh.
(There's a stick of dynamite nearby.)

Yet sadness is her leitmotif, xiv
a sorrowing for someone gone.
(This is what makes her, beyond belief,
exquisite, her face from an icon
surrounded by goldleaf, her skin
illuminated, lit from within.)
Semi-nude, she is transformed.
(Has a sturdy castle been stormed?
Is Cathleen selling her own soul
to save the souls of Blackwater?
Can love stop the manslaughter,
that apocalyptic drum roll?)
Here's a life laid down hour by hour,
immortalized by art, layer by layer.

Messaline and gauze of aerophane. *xv*
(Elements unite in what she wears:
satin weave and water's subtle stain,
ribbed silk of trailing atmospheres.)
A wave of softest grenadine laps
islands of her breasts; tight straps
are flights of coloured forest birds
over backcountry, downwards
flying to valleys of her skirt;
where green fields of chambray
cool her in the great heat of day
when she lies like an idol, inert
yet watchful of the worshipper
in his sunlit temple: her keeper.

Sometimes after a night's work *xvi*
she hardly exists any more;
feels as if she's left London's murk,
been transferred to another shore
unreachable, some world serene,
full of liquid pleasures – a clean
planet – to which only those revert
who on earth have done small hurt,
some prismatic city of crystal
where her nude feet go sliding
on glass-like avenues, surf-riding
through magnificent intercoastal
panoramas and futurescapes:
city that takes a million shapes.

As he, with blazing eyes that train xvii
into her profoundest inner being,
still imitates that bronze plane,
that long vista of her thigh, seeing
where it leads and how to get there
by royal roads and bridges of air,
perspectives and vanishing points.
Another paintbrush he anoints
with pigment from a deck of red,
trying to capture her skintone
where a single sandal strap alone
plunges between her outspread
toes, painted themselves, of course,
a pale-grey tint. (He checks a light source.)

Detail of the Cleavage of Her Toes. xviii
With three more strokes he gets her right.
Another glaze. (He's not one of those
who will give up without a long fight.)
Soon this nocturne will be complete;
he sits down wearily at her feet,
strokes them. (Strange to be outside the skin
he seems to have lived so deep within.)
They fall asleep on the lounge at dawn,
his stained fingers on her kelt jacket,
the coloured into the black-and-white
bleeding: paradiso. 'Yawn ...'
(That was the sun, having a lie-in;
a bland sort of morning, not frying.)

Summer's gone slightly flat: cloud cover. *xix*
Sol snuggles under a grey blanket,
sips gold juice (as an apple lover).
He'll come out later, really spank it.
Big rosy cheeks on fire, Sol smiles.
The Fatman thinks of all those airmiles
earned last night. (Understands one fact:
high romance and destiny attract
the silver dancer of starry rings,
her sickle over the sleeping town:
that thin Corn Moon going down.)
Like golden grain in the Sun King's
granaries, all piled up in dreamtime
twenty-deep, the images that rhyme

One with another – like these who *xx*
sleep – sublime. Again and again,
the same woman, her cheekbones two
wings that lift her face to a high plane;
her lips suggestive of a coastline,
long sensuous curves, white surf, *sunshine*,
when (once or twice) her subtle smile
seems to say: 'Let's give this a while,
not rush under that green breaker yet:
vast wave which must soon collapse,
curving over those whom it traps.
But still, if you wish, let's get wet.'
Gala! (And one she called Salvador,
that man really from l'Age d'Or.)

(A poet who lives all alone xxi
in some small rooftop apartment
lost in London's endless zone,
an emblem of abandonment,
burns himself on a hot plate
at breakfast time, mid-to-late
morning: a finger's roasted.
Immediately, the digit toasted
is raised by reflex to earlobe.
A rapid heat transfer takes place,
no fuss, no plaster and no trace;
no swelling of a reddened globe.
It's not like this with a human heart
reduced to ashes: *a la carte*.)

Awake. Her voice from the balcony xxii
(late afternoon, far end of day's
dense twilight) rising in agony.
He half-deciphers what she says;
lurches from couch to west window.
Beyond, in rain, in evening shadow,
she wears a ripped, terrified smile.
The Grim Reaper's her black mobile
which dark crescent she madly cradles
with one shoulder as she tries to write.
He catches the words: 'Tonight, tonight,
Gatwick, change at Rome.' She huddles.
He sinks to his knees, whispers: 'O God,
You bring down Your titanium rod.'

12

A tragic muse has come to mark i
with slow steps a time and place.
Constant is she to all who embark
on shipwrecked existence; each face
has felt slip down those futile tears
flowing, when the Dark One nears.
There are places laughter can't go;
only weeping is there. 'As you sow,
so shall you reap,' said Jesus Christ.
(I, too, have heard all those jokes:
the Father, Son and Holy Hoax.)
Into darkness we have been enticed.
I like to laugh when laughter comes;
yet I hear those deep sombre drums.

How to end a tragic book, ii
its import and its telling dark?
Is anybody still with me? Look,
I'd try to make the closure less stark,
yet the truth is: we can't change fate.
I'd love to rearrange a mere date,
a few numbers in the march of time,
just draw out that golden prime
when love seemed to want to smile,
make those days live on like a legend.
(Or did I miscomprehend?
Wasn't there an idea for a while
about a Garden of Delights,
somewhere to spend these lonely nights?)

I'll speak of Gala, Parker … Tyg. iii
(Those headlines in the world-press
created so much intrigue
everyone's (you've all) heard, more or less,
McCool's part. The insularity;
the fires; the plunge to insanity;
War Widow, painted in France
in the asylum, his long last glance
at his stricken goddess Gala James.)
It's more painful to talk of her;
I knew Galatea long before
she married, one of my old flames.
You may have to excuse a tear.
She really was something rare.

Her husband Colonel Parker James iv
died in the B'qaa Valley
VX attack, caught in the fumes
that asphyxiated so many.
A greatly valorous man I'm told.
The world shall be very old
when its conundrums are understood.
(And I agree with you: why should
a man of war have no love for God
just because he is a born soldier?)
The world will be even older
when we solve another question, odd:
why is this living so condemned
amid great beauty without end?

Gala flew home with Parker's coffin, v
laid him in the earth at Kimmeridge
not far from Lulworth Cove. (Often
visited early in the marriage
when all was joy. They used to love,
looking at the shooting stars above,
out on the cliffs around that crescent,
where, you know, Keats is everpresent.
Lulworth, the name says it all:
Bright Star, that sonnet, written there,
from the broken poet one last air,
still on Lulworth strand his footfall.)
St Nicholas Church, I remember
Gala read movingly from Homer.

Naturally I was with Elaane. vi
Galatea held up bravely,
she was clearly in so much pain.
(Shortly afterwards, I was gravely
ill; Elaane nursed me back to life,
then, of course, she became my wife.)
At our banns we couldn't track her down;
everyone said she'd just left town.
(She'd broken out of the mandala.)
Then, on the beach (in the West Indies,
one year later?) drinking brandies,
suddenly, from halls of Valhalla:
the goddess who grieved: Mary, Isis,
Star of the Sea – still in crisis? –

Gala, with a child in her arms, vii
with her beautiful baby son
Zhiva. (Perhaps in the Bahamas?)
She played on the sand with him, such fun.
(Not so for the small-islanders,
all those neglected scrublanders
who never see a beach with their eyes
although they do dwell in paradise.
They've heard of sands stretching out
forever under the moonlight
shining on the big hotels so white;
but 'watersport' they think about
sceptically, as some regard harping
angels: 'Just trickery, cardsharping,'

'All lies'. Won't see the West Indies soon, viii
don't like the colonial shadow,
that's just me, a different tune.)
Our old friend was radiant, not low,
yet silent. We didn't really speak;
I chatted with her mother, Veronique,
while Gala and Elaane had a talk.
(Out on the headland took a walk.)
Later on I learned the whole story.
She'd felt tragedy's black wings
strike her, as the hurricane brings
lifewreck. Yet, nothing short of glory,
she was glad to know her boy-child Tyg's.
(At this point my narrative segues.)

When Gala'd agonizedly gone ix
to bring her husband's body home
from chemically stricken Lebanon
(ask not where the VX came from
nobody had real information,
but it marked the escalation)
McCool began his descent
into the pit of permanent
madness. It started with the fires,
an orgy of pyromania.
From his tower of Aquitania,
from his roofdeck, rose inverse spires,
upside down cones of black smoke:
he torched a mountain of his best work.

He lit a nightbeacon up there, x
dragged canvases out of the annexe
(you could see the smoke from Camden Square,
the Grand Union looked Turneresque
at dawn with the conflagration).
The law arrived, the situation
was serious. The tower burned;
no one was hurt; but McCool earned
a lifetime's publicity that day:
'War painter goes on the rampage.'
I saw centrespread, double page
Battlefield in Helmands. They say
all publicity is good publicity –
no way – it was pure toxicity

That day: you could track the stink *xi*
over Hackney Marshes to Lea Bridge.
Perhaps White Cube were tickled pink
when McCool was put in the fridge,
dragged out foaming in handcuffs,
press flash-snapping government toughs
at breakfast time, at break of day,
leading this mythic dude away,
a wildman in chains. 'Tyg McFool'
screamed one odious headline;
on the phone New York said: 'Sign
on the line.' (Into the fire, more fuel.)
Tyg's agent, who shall remain nameless,
signed, made a deal, quite shameless.

A government sanatorium *xii*
near Whitstable (Tyg called it
Unstable) and the sensorium,
radar of world media enthralled. It
hit home with a text. (I've no tv.)
'Mad at last, quick, come bail me
please, they are talking section.'
Things got worse. My recollection:
McCool's full blown mental illness
within that state bedlam began.
(A constable outside caught a fan
in great outrage and sadness
trying to break *in* to the nuthouse;
sadly on film he was so obtuse

People thought him far from the norm xiii
himself.) New York galleries
hunted through ashes, still-warm
embers, thinking of salaries
rising, phoenix-like, from ruin.
It emerged that the harlequin
had put to the torch his latest
series, works perhaps his greatest:
portraits of a mysterious woman;
but had not burned battlepieces,
save one: *War Crime*. So these caprices
on the part of 'the airman'
(a nickname I gave McCool
long years before in artschool)

Did for the whole damn lot then and there. xiv
(That's why it all seemed so Turner,
decline of *The Fighting Téméraire*,
hero worship from the workburner.)
G in Venice, heartbreaking vision;
City of Canals, such precision
wrapped up in mere suggestion:
Her Watercities. Without question
recent masterworks from McCool.
'Delenda est Carthago', some said.
That was right: they're remembered
as one resplendent urban jewel
spiralling up through futuristic skies
haunted by a woman's greenish eyes.

Immortality for McCool, xv
my airman-friend from Aquitaine.
I went to see him twice in Vitrolles,
southwest of Aix, on the train
from Saint Pancras International.
(The Grande Vitesse is sensational,
five hours and you're in the Med,
just arisen from your flying bed.)
Both visits were difficult,
he was quite dissociated,
drugged, possibly opiated,
in a state of mind occult.
I have to say I found it humbling,
he was like God's pure fool stumbling

Through this world without a clue xvi
the first time. On the second visit,
he was more down to earth, knew
me at once, I didn't babysit
as before: he was quite lucid.
Immediately I thought of El Cid
in exile in the torrid south;
untrembling, that proud mouth.
He had his own celebrity suite
in this most expensive loonybin
(in the chateau's oldest wing,
quiet) in every way a complete
island of serenity;
just one sinister amenity:

In our talks he was restrained xvii
(a policy of the asylum).
One to one, he was detained
in an ultraviolet 'labarum'
(strange name given at Vitrolles
to the electronic sensor pool
plotting motion on the ground).
He joked about the haze around
him, faintly ecclesiastical:
'I am the One for whom you have waited.'
(Absolutely the drugs inflated –
gave a heightened, more mystical
dimension to – his conversation.)
We started with some hesitation;

Waded through a dry document xviii
briefly, papers which signified
where matters stood in the event
of non-recovery, all implied.
(I felt the scanners turn unseen,
track behind one way glass screen.)
Then, sensing irritation,
I mentioned his brand new foundation,
a year old: The Parker James Peace Trust.
The warmth of McCool's genius
flashed out: it was instantaneous.
And for a long time we discussed,
in some detail, this achievement,
its evolution and advancement.

After that seminal New York show *xix*
which smashed all records for attendance
(very simply titled *Blow by Blow*)
he'd hit rockbottom. Clairvoyance,
almost, came to the rescue
at that low ebb, when McCool withdrew
to Vitrolles for private treatment,
during international excitement
over 'the swansong of a madman',
'the farewell of a supergiant'.
(On strange drugs he'd become reliant
at 'Unstable'.) A masterplan,
one triste midnight, just came to me:
posthumous solidarity.

A rock 'n' roll friend, John Trailblazer, *xx*
was taking The Serious Road Trip
through the Mafqat, out of Gaza,
calling it 'The Holy Handgrip'.
The idea'd come from Adonai,
to party deep in the Sinai:
Israelis and Palestinians,
DJ's, hand drums, no tensions:
soundtowers pulsing in the desert,
jackals howling at a silver moon
in the Country of Turquoise: madjoun;
drumming-circles at dawn and sunset
on the mountain where Moses exhaled
blue clouds in the tent of meeting, veiled.

I texted (six a.m.) on a high, xxi
by noon we had the transfer cleared;
to Trailblazer's bank I could supply
affirmance from the 'disappeared'
McCool: moonstruck tower-igniter.
('Nightflare McCool', that freedom fighter.)
Two weeks later eight pantechnicons
rolled through Dover – a blue afternoon –
rammed with turntables, generators,
solar powered lightshows (you name it)
pedal powered cinemas (don't tame it).
DJ's and spirits of ancestors
in four wheeled drives all followed
within thirty-six hours. Life mellowed.

Gala was moved, I know, in Sheol. xxii
Tyg painted her one last time
before the final end in Vitrolles:
War Widow, his masterpiece, sublime.
From all memories I take away
McCool's oblique words that day
I first saw him, drugged, in Provence.
(Did he speak of doomed romance?)
'A dead tree in the world's warzone
I rose from dry sands to the south,
drank water, held it in my mouth
for centuries: a heart of stone
flowered, and the sky revealed
the angel of my soul's battlefield.'

NOTES

The action of *McCool* plays out in the spring, summer and autumn of 2011, after a western coalition invasion of the Lebanon.

There is a cosmology of personalities at work in the poem, where McCool himself represents the element of air, liberation and freedom to love; where Parker symbolizes fire-power, will-power and the urge to fight; where Galatea represents water, emotion, sensuality and daring; and where, finally, Elaane stands for the pragmatic element of earth and the processes of judgment and transformation. (An almost invisible narrator – the unnamed poet – represents the fifth element, the quintessence.)

1

The coffee table acts as tympanum to suggest the traditional drums of war. ii

'Down in the dirt.' An airforce expression to describe extreme low flying, the meaning here is connected also with Parker's destiny.

The B'qaa Valley runs roughly north-south through eastern Lebanon, separated by the Anti Lebanon mountain range from Syria. iv

'the cooler heater vest' Though it sounds futuristic the cooler heater vest is a present day hitech military body garment designed to hug the torso tightly so as to achieve maximum effect (through utilization of fluid-carrying tubes in a seamless, poncho-style underjacket). xviii

Dumayr is a city ten or fifteen miles across the Syrian border, southeast of the B'qaa Valley where Colonel James is stationed. xix

Enkidu and the prostitute. Enkidu is the wildman of the Epic of Gilgamesh, captured in the wilderness through the good offices of a temple prostitute who 'tames' this xxii primal nature boy so that he can become a friend to royal Gilgamesh.

(Vide also note to chapter three, stanza xiv 'the cedar forest'.)

2

This sonnet written six months before the credit crunch. i

Halabjah is a predominantly Kurdish city in north-eastern xii
Iraq infamously hit with sarin and VX by Saddam Hussain on the 16th and 17th of March 1998: death-toll, 5,000; with 10,000 seriously injured. Survivors have spoken of a scent of sweet apples from the deadly chemicals dropped by the Iraqi airforce.

White Cube. The celebrated modern art gallery in East xiv
London.

3

dragonskin. This is contemporary military technology, not ii
invention. 'Dragonskin' is the evocative name given to the kevlar armour which renders a modern soldier almost invulnerable to most light-munition attacks. Lightweight silicon discs combine and interlock to protect head and body. Special forces across the world are beginning to be clad in dragonskin (which in turn is now rapidly evolving into 'bio-armour').

McCain. Written before the American election of 2008; in iv
the parallel universe of *McCool* John McCain has won the presidency. The temptation to make this assumption was partially influenced by the Biblical connotations of the American senator's surname. Also influential were the infamous Beachboy-like singing abilities of Senator McCain ('Bomb, Iran; bomb, bomb Iran'.) And last but not least, the mellifluous sonic match and opposition of McCain versus McCool appealed.

Platform of Baalbek. Baalbek is situated at the north end of the B'qaa Valley. Unquestionably (and inexplicably) the most magnificent ruins of the Roman world, the temple complex is dedicated to 'the Heliopolitan triad': Jupiter, Venus and Bacchus. The 'small' temple of the so-called acropolis of Roman Baalbek – the Bacchus temple – is larger than the Pantheon in Rome. Why did the Romans build here? According to venerable Middle Eastern traditions, they constructed their complex on top of the considerably more ancient and even larger scale structure discussed in stanza iv, the legendary 'city of Cain'.

UAV. For unmanned aerial vehicle. v

Yellowcake is the somehow obscene term for weapons- vii
grade plutonium.

the cedar forest. In the Epic of Gilgamesh (the oldest large xiv
scale poem of current civilization) the hero and his wildman friend Enkidu make a perilous journey to the cedar forests of ancient Lebanon, where (perhaps near the great Platform of Baalbek) they encounter what can only be described as a death-dealing automaton monster from the outer realms of science fiction: the dreaded Humbaba.

Titanomachy. Title of a great lost Greek epic, considerably xvi
older than the Iliad and the Odyssey, telling of a mythic war conducted – long before mankind existed – between the Titans and the Olympians.

Baphomet. The idol the Templars were accused of xviii
worshipping, a horned ithyphallic donkey in some depictions.

4 two names of similar sound. Galatea here for the first time viii
realizes the similarity of the names Patrick and Patroclus, the former, her husband's closest friend, the latter, the

great companion of Achilles in the Iliad, killed by Hector. The death of Patroclus is the trigger for the violent climax of the epic.

exposure therapy. Elaane endorses a virtual reality therapy xi
now used in some treatment regimes for those suffering from post-traumatic stress. A self-elaborated representation of any given trauma is digitally stored and replayed incrementally until there is acclimatization to emotional triggers. The technology is new and controversial, with disturbing reports of patients being 'flooded' in attempts to break through pain barriers.

Citizen control television. A play on the CCTV acronym. xvii

5

Maddalena, a small island off the northeastern coast of iii
Sardinia, whose name naturally suggests the Magdalen.

Chicoma mountain-range. The futuristic clinic which Elaane xx
recommends is located in this range just northwest of Santa Fe in New Mexico, above Los Alamos.

6

'discovery of strength'. This term borrowed from Yeats; who i
developed it to describe the phase of the moon's first quarter in his meditation on lunar cyles, *A Vision*, (1925) written in that long period of twenty four years during which the poet resided in Kings Cross.

Drunken moon ... Hay moon ... Thunder moon. These are iii
all folk names – not necessarily from the same cultures – for the moon of July.

Miraval. Raimon de Miraval (1180-1215) is the troubadour xiii
generally considered to have most incarnated the qualities and virtues at the heart of the poetic school of courtly love. The 13th century Catalan troubadour de Bazaudun said of 'Lord Miraval' that 'he knew more

about love than Paris, or any man alive'. The lines quoted are not Miraval's, but represent a compound of an Arabic proverb (with which the troubadour might well have been acquainted in the 12th century) and a piece of fantasy thrown in by the present author.

7 Baselitz. Georg Baselitz (b 1938) the controversial German vi
postmodern painter some of whose work has involved treatment of war themes. He began experimenting with inverted motifs in 1969. Works of Baselitz were shown at White Cube in 2009.

Kali-weed. A Rastafarian name for marijuana (also: xiv
collyweed) a loan term which no doubt filtered into common Jamaican parlance via the fairly large Indian community within the island's population. In subcontinental India, marijuana, or ganja, is sacred to Lord Shiva (whose spouse – in her wildwoman aspect – is the goddess Kali). Even today an intoxicating milk of marijuana (bhang) is administered on special occasions to all worshippers, old and young in Indian temples, though the ancient practice was officially discouraged by the British and has fallen into disuse to a great extent.

9 laughter of the child Astyanax. Perhaps the most emotional v
moment in Homeric literature occurs during a leavetaking of Hector and his wife Andromache (who will see eachother again before Hector is finally slain by Achilles). The Trojan hero is donning his armour on the walls of the city; his wife looks out at the terrifying Greek army and a tragic dialogue begins. Andromache begs her husband not to go into battle. He replies that he could never tolerate her enslavement, that he must fight for their freedom. Tortured words fly back and forth, until Astyanax, Hector's baby son, cradled in

Andromache's arms, scared by the sight of his father's horsehair plume swaying above his war helmet, bursts into tears. At this moment Homer produces the most moving and unexpected resolution. Hector, the man of war – all tenderness suddenly – takes off his helmet and comforts his baby boy, making him chuckle at the crest waving in the sunlight.

someone. Dylan, obviously; 'the singer' was preferred but *vi*
scansion forbade.

A sculpted poppy. The Gate of Bacchus is decorated with, *ix*
among other interesting motifs, poppy capsules. (Tangentially, the inverted poppy capsule has been academically proven – recently – to be the inspiration for the classic Grecian vase. Vide: the 'wild ecstasy' of Keats in 'Ode on a Grecian Urn'.)

It has been speculated that human sacrifice was performed in the Bacchus Temple of the Baalbek complex.

Sufi. The B'qaa valley was one of the main zones for the *xiii*
mass-production of cannabis in the ancient Middle East. (Qinnib in Arabic.) Sufism – the mystical school of Islam – has been linked down the centuries with the sacred use of cannabis, code-named 'the Wine of Haydar' (after a famous Sufi saint much given to consumption of the drug). The town of Qana, in the southern end of the beautiful B'qaa valley, is the gospel story's 'Cana', where Christ turned water into wine at the wedding feast. Modern scholarship has established that there are numerous references to the ritual use of 'kaneh bosm' in the ancient Jewish religion of Moses, as in the New Testament period under the dispensation of Christ.

'jebel'. Elevation, mountain, in Arabic; but also temple *xiv*
mound.

'hiding from the eye of God in vain'. Vide: Victor Hugo's '*La Conscience*' from *Les Légendes des siècles*.

Outremer. Literally 'overseas', the old name for the Crusader xx
states in the Middle East.

10

fullerene glass. A single strand of Carbon 60 the diameter of i
a human hair could hold up the Golden Gate Bridge.

Buckminsterfullerenes – to give these extraordinary molecules their complete and rather oversized name – are the most bonded chemical particles known to science. Every molecule has sixty faces; each face is fused with another face in the chain. Thus the alternative name: Carbon 60. Buckminsterfullerenes – named of course after the visionary American philosopher, Buckminster Fuller, inventor of the geodesic dome – represent the fundamental building blocks of future technology. A jumbo jet made of fullerenes could be picked up in one hand; the problem for designers would be to make the plane heavy enough to fly in a stable manner.

go-pills. The subject of 'the militarization of nature' is vast iii
and disheartening. To succeed in any modern airforce a would-be pilot has to be prepared to become addicted to dexedrine in one form or another: 'speed'. When functioning continually under this dangerous drug for long stretches of time (a stated goal is to train future pilots to endure ten and more days without sleep) concentration becomes superhuman and 'killing-related skills' increase dramatically. When the period of activity ends, 'no-pills' are needed to get the pilot to enter a sleep which lasts many days, effectively a sort of subhuman coma.

Tolstoy. In *Anna Karenina* Tolstoy opines that women are more materialistic than men. This seems to the present author a dangerous half truth. Naturally 'women need things' when motherhood is imminent, and this neediness does condition feminine psychology. But the whole truth is that women are both more materialistic and *more spiritual* than men, being more deeply in touch with the true nature of love. (When an aircraft is crashing, most men will look around for the door marked 'exit' while – it is psychologically proven – women will look for children or the elderly in need of help.) Women represent the golden extremes of sensuality and spirituality, polar opposites which can pull a human being apart and even bring madness; while men, on average (poets possibly excepted), seem to represent compromise, predictable sanity, apparent rationality. v

Two sonnets excised from chapter five depict Elaane enlightening Gala on this subject:

'You stand proud, Scorpio woman,
tortured as you are, torn apart
in the traumatic, superhuman
dark night of a divided heart.
We women are dualistic,
spiritual, materialistic.
We love more; but we *need* more.
With family to feed comes the war
that authorizes Moloch,
justifies all foolishness.
We motivate men to selfishness,
make them overfill – yes, overstock! –
this bank-account, that granary.
O, sweet prostitution's clownery.'

'Seventeen hundred pairs of shoes,
all bought in the name of love? Yeah, right!
To see this truth (which must amuse)
you don't need to have second sight.
Men represent compromise,
life's mediocrities. (Third prize.)
We women are mad – simple as that –
insane as a three-legged cat
with golden extremes of lust
and great pure maternal passion.
(With man's hands he wants to fashion;
he likes to fiddle with the dust.
He's sane, dependable like a mule,
just plods from A to B by the rule.)'

11 Cockaigne. Breughel's painting of the same name elaborates the myth of a city where the residences are made of delicious food; where pigs run through the streets with knives and forks stuck in their backs – not a good town for vegans – and where there exist androgynous monasteries in which monks and nuns live and work under some presumably tantric discipline. Many sources (the great Scottish scholar Lewis Spence among them) link Cockaigne with London. vi

12 'There are places laughter can't go.' The village of Soham was in mind while composing this line. i

Zhiva. Gala and McCool's son is named after the supreme god of Hinduism, Shiva, lord of the dance of life and death. But there's a reference in the altered spelling of the name to the Russian love poet Pasternak whose hero Zhivago proposed and demonstrated that romance could still exist in the reductionist atmosphere of Soviet culture. (In Russian the root 'zhiv' means life, the belly.) vii

Serious Road Trip. The Serious Road Trip performed miraculously in the Balkan conflict when a crew of peacenik London dj's bought an old double-decker bus, and – without a single bulletproof vest in sight – drove heroically into the warzone, partied there and rescued embattled children (the stated intention of their heroic nonviolent direct action). xx

where Moses exhaled. For modern anthropological thinking on the subject of the ritual use of cannabis in both Old Testament and New Testament periods see the work of Sula Benet, the celebrated pioneering Polish academic whose studies of comparative etymology helped her to understand drug-related Hebrew ceremonials in Mosaic, and later in Solomonic, times. Vide also: *The Sacred Mushroom and the Cross* by the controversial British scholar and orientalist, John Allegro.

'the tent of meeting'. The 'mishkan' or tabernacle of Moses, the sanctuary of God, began as a simple tent whose sides were to be saturated with the purest oil of cannabis mixed with frankincense and other ingredients according to the sacred recipes of the Book of Exodus. The tent would then be fumigated with psychotropic smokes and 'meetings with the Divine' would transpire. The 'mishkan' also housed the Ark of the Covenant. There appears no Biblical reference to the tabernacle after the destruction of Jerusalem and the Babylonian enslavement.

A NOTE ON FORM.

McCool is a verse novel told in twelve chapters of twenty-two sonnets, employing the high-speed 'Onegin' stanza of Pushkin, a fourteen-line tetrameter unit rhyming ababccddeffegg.

According to some scholars this stanzaic form can be traced back to the time of the troubadours when serious love poems would be interleaved with lighter, more conversational and zanier material; the idea presumably being to lull the reader into a relaxed and trusting state of mind, and then to strike with tragic or dramatic episodes.

The tetrametric line of *McCool* is syllabically slightly more tolerant than the strict eight-and-nine-count variation that Pushkin allowed himself. Here – with the reader's kind indulgence – will be found a seven syllable line occasionally interspersed.

OF THIS FIRST EDITION OF *McCool* BY AIDAN ANDREW DUN
1000 COPIES HAVE BEEN PRODUCED IN PAPERBACK.
A FURTHER 100 COPIES IN HARDBACK ARE NUMBERED
AND SIGNED BY THE AUTHOR AND CONTAIN TWO CDS
OF THE AUTHOR READING THE ENTIRE WORK,
ALL HOUSED IN A SLIPCASE.
THERE ARE ALSO 15 HORS COMMERCE COPIES
NUMBERED I - XV

Also by Aidan Andrew Dun from Goldmark

VALE ROYAL 1995

UNIVERSAL 2002

THE UNINHABITABLE CITY 2005

SALVIA DIVINORUM 2007